THE
BAKING
LIFE OF
AMELIE
DAY

THE BAKING LIFE OF AMELIE DAY

Vanessa Curtis

Curious Fox

First published in 2014 by Curious Fox,
an imprint of Capstone Global Library Limited,
7 Pilgrim Street, London, EC4V 6LB
Registered company number: 6695582

www.curious-fox.com

Designed by Richard Parker and Steven Mead
Illustrations by Jane Eccles

ISBN 978 1 782 02166 7

18 17 16 15 14
10 9 8 7 6 5 4 3 2 1

A CIP catalogue for this book is available from the British
Library.

Printed and bound by CPI Group (UK) Ltd,
Croydon, CR0 4YY

To Trevor and Steve,
with love

Chapter One

There was this poem Mum used to read to me when I was six.

Boys were made up of slugs, snails and puppy-dog tails.

Girls were made up of sugar, spice and all things nice.

You would have thought that I'd given Mum the evil eye when she read that bit out. I'm famous at school for having attitude and ranting on about how girls are just as good as boys. I play in the girls' football team and we thrashed the boys only last week so you can see what I mean.

But that poem must have somehow stuck in my head or got through my skin and into my body.

If you cut my arm I reckon it's not blood you'll see pouring out, but pure cane sugar.

If you look into the whites of my eyes you'll see that they're the tiniest bit yellow. Like the palest, freshest sponge cake made with plenty of free-range eggs.

Even my hair is the colour of dark melted chocolate swirling around a glass bowl on a pan of hot water which is gently simmering beneath.

I am so made up of sugar and spice.

I live to bake. My life would be empty without it.

Most of the time there's only one thing on my mind: Flour Power.

Mum's got used to her kitchen being a complete mess.

'If it keeps you happy,' she says through tight lips, casting a horrified eye over her stainless steel surfaces, or what's left of them underneath the smears of flour, egg and butter which mark my residency in the kitchen.

'Mm,' I say, but I'm never really listening. I'm greasing a couple of cake tins with a slip of buttery paper and lining them with silver foil.

'What is it today?' says Mum, checking her lipstick in the mirror and pressing her lips together. Mum works for a solicitor and always has to wear a suit and full make-up by eight each morning.

'Orange polenta muffins,' I say, creaming sugar and butter together in Mum's brown pottery bowl and then pouring white flour into my grandmother's Victorian weighing scales. I reckon they're pretty neat. Mum was going to chuck them into a skip, but I rescued them and polished them up until they gleamed as black and shiny as treacle.

'Wow, very twenty-first century,' says Mum. 'I'm not sure I even know what to do with polenta.' She picks up her black handbag with the gold chain and takes one last look in the mirror. There's a hoot from outside. Mum's friend Yvonne always drives her into work. They share an office and do an awful lot of boring women's stuff, like sharing bottles of wine together over lunch and going shopping for shoes.

'It's a grain,' I say. 'You get it in the supermarket. Adds a moist texture so that you can add less flour. It should soak up the orange juice. If you undercook it you get too much crunch, though.'

'Oh, right,' says Mum, but she's halfway out of the door. I can see Yvonne squirting gallons of perfume on at the wheel. She's always running slightly late. 'Don't forget to go to school, Amelie! And don't forget to take all your stuff, you know?'

I frown.

I do know.

I'm not likely to forget.

Then she slams the door and clicks off in her heels. I hear the screech of her greeting Yvonne, then another slam and the sound of the car disappearing off into the distance.

I wipe my hands on a tea towel and crank up the volume on the radio. Then I glance at the kitchen clock.

Forty minutes before I need to leave for school. Perfect timing.

I pour the juice of four freshly squeezed oranges into my mixture and add the grated orange peel. Then I raise the dripping wooden spoon to my mouth and allow the raw mix to swish around my mouth a bit.

My tongue comes alive with zingy orange and rich,

buttery sponge mix.

'Awesome,' I say, reaching for a metal spoon. I spoon the mixture into two greased muffin tins and slide them into the oven.

Then I bolt upstairs to get ready for school.

I leave a tray of muffins cooling on the rack for Mum to see when she gets home. She works part-time so she's always home before me. I put the rest into a Tupperware box and shove it into my schoolbag.

Then I pick up the plumpest one from the rack, dollop a spoonful of rich, creamy Greek yoghurt on the top and stuff it into my mouth as I run for the school bus. Crumbs and yoghurt go all over my school uniform but I don't care. School is only of secondary importance. I spend the whole day in class dreaming up recipes that I can try out when I get home. I've even got a job in the local grocer's shop in town. I asked to be paid in ingredients which made Karim, the owner of the shop, look closely at me over the top of his black glasses and scowl until his hairy eyebrows met in the middle, like two confused beetles.

'You want me to pay you in eggs and flour?' he said. 'This is most unusual. Girls your age like money for make-up and boys, no?'

His shoulders moved up and down when he laughed. Then he stopped because I wasn't laughing back. I mean – I do like clothes and make-up and stuff as much as the next thirteen-year-old girl, but I'm not obsessed with them like I am with baking.

'Flour, eggs, sugar and butter with other ingredients thrown in according to season,' I say in my best business-like voice. 'That's the deal. Take it or leave it.'

Karim rubbed his brow in astonishment and shook his head.

'You are one crazy English girl,' he said. 'But OK. I pay you in stuff. Not too much, mind.'

I skipped all the way home on the day I got the job at Karim's shop.

School's OK.

I sit next to Gemma Smith, my best friend and guinea pig.

She's not actually a guinea pig. What I mean is that I test out all my new recipes on her before I write them into *The Amelie Day Book of Baking*. The book is going to be published one day and be a mega-best-seller.

Gemma and I are total opposites which I guess is why we've been best friends for nearly three years. She's tall, blonde and pink-cheeked. She loves clothes, jewellery and animals. I'm short, dark and sallow-skinned and animals make me cough.

At break-time I get out my plastic box and hoist myself up onto the desk next to Gemma. I waft the box under her nose until she caves in and takes one of the fat muffins out of the box.

'Orangey,' she says, sniffing. 'Yum. Did you make these today?'

I nod and take another one for myself.

'Yeah, course,' I say. 'You know me.'

Gemma stuffs in the muffin with a faraway look in her eyes.

'These are the best muffins ever,' she says, all loyal.

I laugh. She says that about every single batch that I make. The laugh turns into a cough. Gemma rubs my back.

'OK?' she says. I take a deep steadying breath and nod.

'Polenta,' I choke. 'That's what gives them the moist texture.'

'Mmm,' says Gemma. 'Could I have another one for lunch?'

I let her take two and then I eat another one myself, straight down in three bites.

Most people wouldn't stay as slim as I am if they ate all the cake and calories I stuff down every day.

Most people would get fat and spotty and probably die.

But then again, as Mum is always reminding me, I am not Most People.

I snap the lid of my box shut.

'French,' I say, as the bell goes.

I link arms with Gemma and head off towards class.

At lunchtime I hang out with Harry. I think we might be going out. Harry's brilliant. He just accepts me for who I am. I can't even remember my life without Harry in it, because I've grown up with him since we were six years old. At one point, his parents lived next door to mine so he truly was the 'boy next door.' He's in the year above me at school.

And he's a big fan of my baking.

'Awesome,' he says, biting down on one of my orange muffins with a glint in his dark brown eyes. I reckon a lot of the other girls wish they were going out with Harry. He's handsome, but not in an arrogant way, more a sporty, fit kind of way.

And he's kind.

'You OK today?' he's saying.

I flush a little. Wish people wouldn't keep asking me that. I know it's only because he cares but it makes me feel like some charity case sometimes.

'Fine,' I say. I wave the plastic box of muffins under his nose and Harry doesn't take much persuading to help himself to another one.

Then I head off to my next class in order to disguise another bout of coughing.

I leave Harry stuffing his face and waving.

When I get home Mum is pacing up and down by the window.

She's still wearing her black suit but she's taken off her high pointy shoes and replaced them with pink slippers, which is a bit of an odd look, kind of like two mothers rolled into one.

'This might be it!' she says, waving a bit of paper in the air just out of my reach and whisking it away every time I try to grab it.

I frown. I'm really tired and I want to get my homework done fast so that I can invent some more recipes. All day in school I've been seeing chocolate sauce and pink mini-marshmallows in my head and now I want to try out an idea for cupcakes.

'Mother,' I say, pulling my long hair back from my hot face, 'just stop clowning around and give me the letter, will you?'

Mum looks at my flushed face and her teasing smile becomes one of concern.

'You look a bit wiped out, love,' she says. 'Sit down. I'll get you a drink.'

She tosses the letter onto my lap and goes into the kitchen.

I look down at the envelope with my name on it and my heart does lots of flips and jumps and pains like little stitches.

It's only a letter, I tell myself. It's not going to bite me.

And even if it doesn't contain the news that I want, it's not like my whole life is going to be ruined, is it?

Well – no more than it already has been by other stuff.

I tell myself lots more comforting and reassuring things but the other bit of me isn't listening.

The other bit of me is dead ambitious. It's jumping up and down and screaming, 'You've got to get this, you've got to get this!' over and over again.

I pick up the narrow white envelope and slit it open with my fingernails.

I pull out the folded piece of A4 paper and skim it with one eye shut. Like that's going to make any difference.

Then I clutch at my heart and yell for Mum.

Tangy Orange Polenta Muffins

To make 16 of these nice, orangey little muffins you will need:

    250g (9 oz) of unsalted butter

    250g (9 oz) of golden caster sugar

    4 large eggs

    140g (5oz) of polenta (this is a maize flour that you can find in the supermarket in the rice/pasta/foreign foods aisles)

    200g (7oz) of plain flour

    2 teaspoons of baking powder

    The zest and juice of two large oranges (you need to hold back 100ml (½ a cup) for the glaze)

For the glaze:

    100ml (½ a cup) orange juice

    100g (3 ½ oz) golden caster sugar

So you need to heat the oven up first before you put anything in it. Heat it to 160°C/320°F/gas mark 3 (140°C/280°F/gas mark 1 if you are using a fan oven). If the butter is hard as a block of ice, put it in the oven in a bowl for a few minutes to soften it up, because there's nothing worse than trying to mix hard butter with sugar – it will make you grumpy and cross.

You'll also need a muffin tin (or possibly two if you only have 12 holes in each) and some muffin baking cases. You can get all this stuff in the supermarket. Put a cake case in each of the holes in the tins and set this all aside.

When your butter is melted, cream it together with the 250g of golden caster sugar. When I say 'cream' I mean beat together with a wooden spoon, if you happen to have one. When it's all light and fluffy then add in one large egg at a time, beating hard in between.

Once that's all done, mix in all the dry ingredients (flour, baking powder, polenta) and add in the zest (which is the outside of the peel – you can 'zest' with a special gadget which your mum or dad probably has in their kitchen, or with a grater) and the juice of the two large oranges (you can either squeeze them to death or use a special juicing gadget, which, again, you might have in a kitchen drawer somewhere). Remember to keep back 100ml of the juice for your glaze later.

OK, so by now you probably have one of the most gloopiest and delicious cake mixes on the planet – it should be pale orange and tasty. Time to dollop it into the muffin cases using a spoon – fill them nearly to the top but not quite. Then put them into the middle shelf of your hot oven and set the timer for about 25 minutes, or until they're all nice and golden on top and risen.

While they're baking you could make the orange syrup, which is really easy. Just boil up 100ml of your orange juice with 100g of golden caster sugar and then let it simmer (on a lower heat) for only five minutes. When you've taken your cakes out of the oven and removed the paper cases, stick a spoon in the syrup and dribble a load of it over the top of the cakes.

Allow them to cool down and then serve them with a luscious dollop of crème fraiche or natural yoghurt, or you could even try adding some ice cream. They taste even better the next day. Don't ask me why, but they do.

Chapter Two

I can't believe it.

'I'm through!' I yell, over and over. Mum throws her arms around me and we do an excited victory dance around the lounge, until we're both out of breath and have to sit back down.

'Let me look at it again,' says Mum. She re-reads the letter for about the millionth time. 'I'm so proud of you, Amelie. You did it!'

I lean my head back against the sofa. I feel as if I've been punched in the chest and head. It's the relief, after all the months of waiting to get the letter after I sent in my application.

'You should frame that,' says Mum. She sits down next to me and we both gaze at the logo on the top of the letter.

Britain's Best Teen Baker of the Year Competition.

I've made it through to the quarter-finals.

That means I'm in with a real chance of World Cake Domination.

'Hooray,' I say in a tired voice. Then I flop down and text Gemma the good news.

Mum kisses the top of my head.

The letter says I have to travel up to London for the quarter-finals. There's going to be a big competition, based in a trendy glass-fronted building designed especially for it and the whole thing is going to be filmed for a few television programmes too.

I'll be taking part in a bake-off against twelve other teenagers and the three winners will end up in the semi-finals. After that one person will be eliminated and only two will be left in the Grand Final to fight it out for the title of Britain's Best Teen Baker of the Year.

I've got to come up with my own recipes for the quarter-finals and it has to be a mixture of cakes and biscuits too, just to show that I'm not a one-cake pony. I've got to do two baked desserts and one selection of biscuits.

I'm a bit worried about the biscuits. I mean – I DO know how to make biscuits and they always taste good, but I need something really unusual for the competition and, to be honest, I'm more at home with making cakes. There's something about swirling a spoonful of gloopy white icing across the top of a fragrant little chocolate cake that hits about 100 on my cakeometer.

'I need books,' I say to Mum. 'Pronto. I mean – I need them like yesterday. Could I have some money?'

'What about your shop job?' says Mum. 'Or have they stopped paying you?'

I sigh. I've told Mum about a million times that I don't get paid in actual cash. Just at this moment I rather wish that I did. Then I could rush into town and fill my arms with as many baking books as I could get my hands on.

'I'm skint,' I say. 'I need money. Please, Mum? Could I have an advance on my pocket money? It's really important.'

Mum sighs and reaches for her handbag. My heart lifts up, all hopeful.

Then she zips it shut again. My heart plummets back down into my boots.

'I've got a better idea,' she says. 'And a cheaper one. Why don't you get onto one of your social networking sites and make an appeal for recipes?'

I roll my eyes and cross my arms. Underneath, my brain starts to compute in a wild and furious way quite at odds with how my knackered body is feeling.

I don't want to give Mum the satisfaction of knowing that her idea is actually really awesome, so I skulk off to my bedroom and then I dash to my laptop and log on.

I go onto Facebook and I write to all my friends on there, asking if they could send me any recipes for savoury stuff. Then I rewrite my request because I realise that most of my friends aren't quite as obsessed with baking as I am, so I ask them to ask their parents for recipes too. Then I set myself up a blog where I can update people with all the news from the competition and after loads of thought

I write my first blog entry and post it live. This is what it says:

If you've found this website it might be because you've Googled the work 'cake' or the word 'bake', or maybe you're just nosing around on the internet and have found me by accident. Anyway, welcome to the first blog posting of Amelie Day, wannabee Champion Baker and future author of *The Amelie Day Book of Baking*. I've been chosen as a quarter finalist in *Britain's Best Teen Baker* and I'll be appearing on a television screen near you in the not-too-distant future. I live with my Mum but not my Dad. They split up when I was two but they're still friends, or so they say. Mum is a big fan of my baking, for various reasons which I'm not going to list here 'cos they're boring and my whole life is too full of them anyway. But all you need to know is that I bake. I love baking. It's my life. Flour Power! Oh, and I need your recipes, especially if you know how to make any really awesome and unusual biscuits. So if you've got any you don't mind sharing with me, please post them here.

I stand back and read my first blog posting. Then I read it again with my mouth full of chocolate. I keep emergency rations in my schoolbag and in my desk drawer at home. Most kids are told not to stuff themselves with junk all the time, but I'm not most kids and my mum doesn't mind.

Besides, my chocolate is really good quality. I don't buy so much of the rubbish sugary milky stuff that other kids are addicted to, although from time to time it's the only thing that will do when I'm desperate for a quick pick-me-up sugar/calorie fest.

I watched a programme about how real, decent chocolate comes from the best quality cacao beans and I persuaded Karim to order a few bars of the dark stuff for his shop, knowing full well that the other customers wouldn't go near it. He ended up with the bars leftover unsold, so guess what? He passed them straight to me as part of my 'wages'.

I've got some left in my emergency stash drawer. I slide it out of the pale silver wrapper and enjoy the snapping sound that it makes when I break it. I read in a cookbook once that this is a sign of really good chocolate. Then I sniff the rich smell of the beans. It's a sharp smell, a bit like lemons. I put one precious square onto my tongue and allow it to melt without sucking. It zings into my mouth and seems to wake up my brain. I sit back in my chair with a big sigh and enjoy the sensation. When it's gone, I don't replace it. Sometimes a little bit is loads more delicious than a lot.

I only learned that quite recently. It kind of goes against everything that Mum is telling me to do all the time, but I reckon that the odd day where I don't over-eat is probably not going to do me much more harm than has already been done.

I log off from my computer and go downstairs to see what Mum is making for dinner.

~

'You'll need some new clothes,' Mum says.

We're eating Shepherd's Pie together at the kitchen table with the doors thrown open onto the courtyard outside. Our house used to be part of an old stable for a grand estate. The grand house has long since gone, but the stable buildings were converted into houses years ago and we live on the very end of the block. Next to our house is a huge arch where the horses and carriages used to pass through into the back of the grand estate, but nowadays cars drive through it to park outside their houses instead. If you look closely up at the arch you can still see hinges where the grand gates once were and our house is full of beams with old nails hammered through them for holding horse tack and harnesses. It's what Mum calls a 'character property' when she's describing it to people she doesn't know. It's damp in winter, has low ceilings and tons of leaks, but the brilliant thing is that it's got an enormous kitchen made up of three rooms knocked through into one. There's a cooking station in the middle with stools around the outside where we eat meals, do homework or in my case, bake myself into oblivion.

Mum got the house when she and Dad got divorced. Dad came from a rich family, so he was generous when they split up and even came round house-hunting with her until she laid eyes upon the run-down stable conversion where we now live. He paid her extra to have it done up and we've been here for eleven years.

I love our house, but most of all I love the kitchen.

That's where my heart belongs.

That's where I truly feel at home.

'I don't need any more clothes, Mum,' I say.

My mind isn't on clothes tonight. Or any night, come to think of it.

I just logged onto my blog and already there are two recipes on there from complete strangers who've found it. One of them, from a girl called Jane, is for chocolate chip and peanut cookies. My eyes light up and I print off her recipe and I'm trying to read it downstairs, but Mum keeps interrupting me.

'Yes, but don't you want to look nice on the television?' asks Mum. She glances at my purple leggings and white t-shirt with a giant picture of a purple cupcake in the middle of it. 'You look lovely when you make the effort, Amelie.'

She comes over to where I'm sitting, forking up carrots and mince, and pulls my hair back onto the damp nape of my neck.

'I wish you'd wear your hair up instead of in this bird's nest,' she says, releasing it back into its usual scruffy position. 'You have a fabulous profile. Like a French actress or something.'

I bat her away with my hands. 'Mum,' I say. 'I'm so not in the mood. It's more important that I actually know what I'm going to cook for this competition, isn't it?'

Mum sighs and loads empty plates into the dishwasher.

'Well, I'm going to take you shopping at the weekend,' she says. 'No argument. I got paid a little bonus last week and I think we both deserve a treat.'

'OK, OK,' I say. 'Whatever. And now I need to go and experiment with golden syrup, if that's alright with you?'

Mum turns round with a plate in her hand.

'Amelie,' she says. 'We need to talk about how we're actually going to manage this trip to London. I mean – it's going to be tough on you.'

It's on the tip of my tongue to be rude, because I hate it when she makes a fuss. I guess I know that it all comes from years of caring and worrying about me, so I bite my tongue and go over to the kitchen cupboard where I've labelled the door 'AMELIE'S STUFF'.

I stare at all the lovely rows of tins and jars and bottles and packets, but my eyes appear to have misted over or got tired or something, because for a moment I can't see.

Then the mist clears.

I grab a tin of golden syrup and prise open the lid with the end of a teaspoon.

I spend the rest of the evening trying not to think about what Mum just said.

Chapter Three

We hit town on Saturday. I've brought Gemma with for moral support. Mum tends to get a bit carried away when confronted with the joy of frocks and shoes. Mind you, Gemma loves that sort of thing as well, so I'm not expecting much help from her either.

Mum heads into the very first clothes shop that we come across.

'I don't even LIKE their stuff,' I groan, but Mum has developed her usual selective deafness and is throwing armfuls of dresses over her arm and rifling through racks and shelves with a determined frown on her face.

'This would be a lovely colour on you, Gemma,' she says, holding up a pale yellow strappy dress in thin cotton against Gemma's pink skin and blonde hair. 'Wouldn't suit Amelie though. She needs bolder colour against her dark hair.'

'Actually, Mrs Day, I really love that,' says Gemma, spinning round and holding the dress up against her in front of the mirror. 'But Mum hasn't actually given me my pocket money yet, so…'

She affects a sad look and puts the dress back on the rail. Gemma knows how to play my mother like a pack of cards. She comes from a single-parent family, just like me, but her mother only has a small job in a supermarket and there isn't much money left for clothes. Gemma and her mum always come to us for Christmas dinner every year so that Mum can make a big fuss of them and show off her huge kitchen all at the same time.

It's worked, as usual.

'Oh Gemma,' says Mum, putting an arm around my best friend. 'If you love it, then you shall have it! I got a bonus last week.'

She gives Gemma a note and gestures at her to go and pay for the dress. I swear that my friend actually SKIPS to the cash till.

I shudder and give Mum my disapproving look, but I can't help smiling. She's a cool mum, most of the time.

When she's not fussing over me, that is.

'And what about a dress for you?' Mum is saying. 'Come on! You might get through to the final, you never know! Then there will be millions of people watching your every move on television.'

When she says this, I get a butterfly thrill in my stomach. That leads me to think about butterfly cakes, the ones with the little sponge wings that you place on top in the buttercream. I'm so wrapped up in thinking about whether I could incorporate blueberry syrup that I don't even really notice when Mum shoves an armful of dresses onto me and pushes me into a changing room.

The dresses are all vile. I hate dresses anyway. Although I've got long dark hair and a girly sort of face, I'm not really into pretty dressing. I like leggings, jeans, boots and denim or leather jackets best of all.

In the end I reach a compromise with Mum and I agree on a sleeveless tunic with a grey and white pattern on it and some cropped black leggings and a pair of black ballerinas. It all kind of goes with my hair and colouring, so she's happy enough and I can't wait to get out of the shop and go home.

I'm starting to feel a bit weird.

I glance in the mirror as we leave the shop with our parcels. My skin has gone sort of grey with a slight bluish tinge. I try to walk ahead of Mum so that she doesn't notice, but Mum is trained in the art of monitoring my health at all times and she has some sort of psychic radar which now causes her to catch me up and stare straight into my face.

'You don't look too good,' she says, dropping her bags and putting both hands on my shoulders. 'Surely you can't be getting another infection? You're on enough antibiotics to make you rattle!'

My head starts to swim and my chest tightens up.

'Uh-oh,' says Gemma, who knows the signs almost as well as Mum does. 'Should I get somebody?'

Mum has ushered me back into the shop and pushed me into a chair. A concerned shop assistant hovers behind her. A crowd appears to be gathering. Wow. I must look really bad.

'Inhaler,' I choke. My mother reaches into her huge bag and pulls out a small plastic blue device and passes it to me. I take several deep puffs but it's not enough to stop the cough coming.

I bend over double and cough like I'm trying to cough my heart out of my body. Sometimes it feels as if I might actually succeed. That would be gross. Imagine coughing your heart out of your mouth. Ew.

'Take it easy,' Mum is saying. She's crouching down in front of me now. Her tan has faded and her face looks all papery and old. 'Gemma, could you get the water out of my bag, love?'

Gemma passes over the bottle with a solemn look on her pale face. Her new yellow dress lies forgotten in its bag on the floor.

I gulp at the water and cough some more and then at last the choked-up feeling in my chest subsides a bit as the inhaler kicks in and does its work.

'Wow,' I say, wiping my eyes. 'I felt fine when we got here.'

'Hmm,' says my mother, pushing my hair back off my face. 'I'm really not sure that we should even be thinking about going to London for this competition, Amelie. A week spent in Central London with the pollution and everything in the middle of summer. No – it's a crazy idea.

I think I'm going to have to go back on what I said. We can't go to London, and that's that.'

My eyes are watering again as we walk in silence out of the shop. This time it's not the coughing that's done it, but the sinking feelings of gloom and disappointment that are threatening to engulf me.

Mum opens the car doors in silence. Gemma slides in next to me on the back seat and gives me sympathetic looks but she doesn't dare speak. She fingers the plastic bag with her dress in. I can tell that she's dying to look inside but doesn't want to appear uncaring.

I spend the journey home with my head buried in my hands.

I hate this stupid illness and what it does to my life.

Oh. I didn't explain, did I? What's wrong with me, I mean.

I suffer from an illness called Cystic Fibrosis.

There is no cure for it at the moment.

This basically means, I'm going to die.

Chapter Four

When I say I'm going to die, I don't mean right away.

Lots of people with Cystic Fibrosis now go on into adulthood. I met somebody at the hospital who was nearly forty and to me that seemed pretty ancient, so I was impressed.

I've had the illness since I was born. You get it if both your parents carry a faulty gene and it looks like mine did. I know that Mum still blames herself whenever I get more unwell which is stupid really, because I don't blame her and how could she have known about carrying the faulty gene? I got diagnosed before my first birthday after Mum noticed that whenever she kissed me, she could taste salt. People with CF produce more salt when they sweat. So they gave me the sweat test and told Mum that I had the illness.

Having Cystic Fibrosis means that there are two big

problems I have to live with on a daily basis.

The first is that my lungs fill up with mucus and I feel like I'm going to choke. I have ways of treating this at home or in hospital, but it takes up masses of time and that's a right pain. The other frustrating thing is that my digestive system doesn't work as well as it should do and I can't digest my food properly. I have to take special capsules called enzymes with every single meal I eat, otherwise I get a vile stomach ache and might throw up.

There are upsides of having Cystic Fibrosis though. I'm allowed to stuff my face! So for lunch I can have cheese sandwiches and crisps and a thick milkshake and that's just for starters. I snack throughout the day on crisps and biscuits and the teachers make an exception for me because they know if I don't eat enough I'll keel over and then my mother will come rampaging down to the school and have a go at them.

The weird thing is that even though I eat masses of crap and I'm underweight, my skin is clear and glowing. Gemma gets really annoyed about that. She eats salad for lunch every day and gulps juice but she's got masses of spots.

'I don't get it,' she says. 'You practically LIVE off cake. How come your complexion is so good?'

I smile and look superior whenever she says this. Well – with Cystic Fibrosis you have to take all the compliments you can, whenever you can get them.

I struggle to keep looking good. It's one of the things about CF that I really hate. Yeah, I can eat whatever I like whenever I like, but the downside is that despite all that, I'm still really underweight and bony. I'm quite short, too, as CF stops you growing to the same height as everybody else.

Gemma reckons I'm pretty, though.

'Your hair is to die for,' she said once. Unfortunate words to use, but I laughed anyway. My hair is almost black and very long and shiny. 'And you've got a heart-shaped face.'

It's true. I do have an OK sort of face. It's just my body that lets me down.

For all the things going wrong inside of me I take tablets. Hundreds and hundreds of them. Some of my medicine is inhaled from the nebuliser, but much more of it comes in the form of tablets.

Every morning Mum hands me a box with the days of the week written on little plastic compartments and I open my mouth and gulp down a handful of tablets with a glass of water. This is what I take:

Tablets to open my airways up.

Tablets to stop acid coming up from my stomach and burning my throat.

Multivitamins to keep my general health levels as high as possible.

Tablets to help my body break down fats.

Tablets to help me breathe easier through my sinuses.

Vitamin K for bone strength.

Antibiotics to stop chest infections.

I take all of these more than once a day. Mum counted them up and told me that I take seventy-five pills every single day.

So.

As luck would have it, my growing up with Cystic Fibrosis started to coincide with my love of baking, and seeing as how I need to get in at least 3000 calories per day, it seems like the perfect career to be aiming for. Even Mum can't really argue with that. I reckon she secretly wanted me to train to be something like an accountant and earn loads of money, but now I'm on the path to world cake domination she's wise enough to see that she can't really stop me.

Nothing and nobody can get in the way of my ambition now.

I'm determined to get to London, whatever Mum says.

I'm going to bake my way to the top.

Flour Power!

You might think that people with Cystic Fibrosis can't really make proper relationships.

You'd be wrong.

Harry's really cool about the whole thing.

I've had it all the time I've known him, which is ages. But when we started going out I reminded him that life with a CF patient isn't exactly fun.

'I hang out at hospitals a lot,' I said. 'If you're looking for a bouncy person with lots of breath, you'd be better off asking Gemma out instead.'

There.

I gave him every chance to back off and run away in horror from the crazy sick girl with the bag full of cake and the ribcage which poked through her t-shirt.

Instead he reached out and took my hand.

I was so surprised that I lost the power of speech.

Not for long though.

'Did you hear what I said?' I said. 'I'm not always a lot of fun.'

Harry continued to hold my hand and stare into my eyes. Inside my chest there were little flutterings and leaps and for once it was nothing to do with excess mucus production or the beginnings of some vile infection.

'So?' he said. 'We've all got to die sometime, right? Any of us could die tomorrow. I reckon it's no big deal.'

I continued to stare at him in amazement. I thought that most boys wouldn't want a girlfriend who spends much of her free time coughing, puking, fainting, being hooked up to an antibiotic drip or puffing on an inhaler, but then again Harry seems to not be most boys, in the same way that I am not most girls.

'Anyway,' he said. 'You make awesome cakes. And I kind of like to eat a lot of cake. So I reckon we ought to go out sometime, yeah?'

I looked into his dark eyes and at his brown floppy hair and from that moment on I was smitten.

'I will be your Cake Tester,' he said as he left. 'You can try out all your recipes on me.'

That did it for me. We've been together ever since.

I'm sitting in the local park with Harry and a big wicker basket that I've stolen from Mum.

It's a beautiful day. Kids are playing on the swings and mothers are standing around in little huddles gossiping or eating ice creams.

I'm feeling a bit deflated, even though it's great being with Harry on a Sunday with the sun beaming down and the whole day ahead of us.

Mum isn't budging on the whole London thing. She took me to the GP the day after my collapse in the clothes shop and he said that it might be that my lung function has decreased. I won't know for sure until my annual review, but Mum has been tasked with forcing me to rest, take extra medication and have early nights.

That means that I've had to cut down playing matches with the football team at school, at least for a while. It's a pain, because when you've got Cystic Fibrosis it's really important to take loads of exercise to keep your lungs working as well as they can, but I'm getting too out of breath to run around the pitch at the moment. It also means that I've stopped revising for my exams quite as hard as I had been. I still do the work but I go to bed earlier or else Mum starts yelling swear words up the stairs.

Mum is very fond of Harry. I heard her whispering to him about my current state of health as we left the house, but I pretended not to notice. It's kind of embarrassing – Harry can see how well I am just by looking at me, so there's no need for Mum to be all extra anxious and over-motherly, but I don't reckon I'll ever stop her.

'Sausage roll?' I say, offering Harry the first of about twenty plastic boxes from Mum's picnic hamper.

Harry's eyes light up. He's not at all overweight or anything but he does love food. Most of it gets burned off during rugby tournaments or by cycling. Harry is very into his sports.

'Made by you?' he says. 'Stupid question. Of course they are made by you.'

He sinks his teeth into the warm, greasy puff pastry and closes his eyes for a moment.

'Awesome,' he says. 'Best I've ever had.'

I kind of know he's not lying, either. I've perfected my sausage rolls over the last year by using top-quality flour and free-range pork mince bought from the local butcher out of my pocket money from Mum. I reckon I've achieved just the right balance between moist, savoury meat and crisp, flaky pastry. I've brought two little jars of yellow-brown French mustard from a market I went to with Mum last time we were on holiday. Harry spoons the mustard all over another sausage roll and bites into it with his usual enthusiasm.

I'm less hungry today. My chest is tight and the stronger antibiotics that the GP has just put me onto to avoid another chest infection make me feel a bit sick. I pass up on the sausage rolls and fiddle about looking for cake instead. Somehow it's always easier to eat sweet stuff when I'm feeling ill.

I snap open the lid and peer inside. Four perfect chocolate cupcakes nestle up like newborn kittens in a box, waiting to be chosen. The chocolate frosting on top glistens in the sun.

I select the special one I've made for Harry and pass it over.

'Aw,' he says. 'That's sweet. Cheers, Mel.'

Harry always calls me Mel. He reckons 'Amelie' isn't really a name that suits me and he may well be right. He also says it reminds him of a really long, dull French film that his mother forced him to watch once.

'It was all slow motion doors swinging back and forth,' he said. 'Bo-ring.'

He's picking the tiny red heart from the top of his cupcake and popping it in his mouth. I had the heart idea this morning when I looked in my special cupboard and found a forgotten roll of fondant icing. Fondant icing is kind of cheating and I prefer to make my own, but it's useful to colour and make into shapes, so that's what I did.

I made Mum one of the special heart cakes as well and left it in the kitchen for her to find. Even though we're kind of not speaking over all this London stress, I still reckon that she deserves a cake.

Mum has gone through a lot over the course of the last thirteen years.

I suppose it can't be easy having a child with my illness to look after, even though I'm not really going to be a child for much longer.

It's why she and Dad stayed on good terms, too. They decided that it wouldn't do me any good to live between two warring, battle-scarred and bitter parents, so they made a pact to stay friends for my sake and they've pretty much managed it ever since.

'Could I have another one?' Harry is saying. He's gazing into the cake box. 'These are my favourites, deffo.'

I smile and pass it over. Then I force down another one myself. Got to keep the calories going in.

If I keep eating and get stronger again, maybe Mum will let me go to London and take part in the competition.

'I hope so,' says Harry. I didn't realise I'd spoken my last sentence out loud. 'I know how much you want to get there. I'll come with, if you like.'

I smile and let him take my hand, but my eyes are focused on the dark grey storm cloud threatening to pass over the sun and ruin our lazy picnic.

I don't feel so good today.

What if my lung function goes downhill?

What if I end up in hospital again instead of taking part in the competition?

I shudder.

Sometimes having Cystic Fibrosis seems a bit like someone's having a bad joke with me.

Most of the time I try to stay positive. Mum's always made a big deal out of telling me that I'm special and asking me who wants to be like everybody else anyway.

'You're unique,' she says. 'And you have unique creative talents, too.'

Yeah. But there's not much point having the talents if I can't do anything about them, is there?

For the first time in ages, I wish that I was normal.

Like Gemma, like Harry.

Just like everybody else.

Best Ever Sausage Rolls

To make about 25 of these gorgeous mouthfuls you will need:

1 tablespoon butter

1 red onion, peeled and finely sliced

A sprig of fresh sage leaves or another green herb like parsley or thyme

A handful of breadcrumbs

6 good pork sausages

300g (10 ½ oz) of defrosted puff pastry. (It's pretty hard work making your own puff pastry. The stuff you can buy in the supermarket tastes just as good and is much easier to use. You can get this in the freezer cabinets in the supermarket.)

1 egg

A little bit of milk

So you need to heat the oven up to the temperature it says on the puff pastry packet. Then melt the butter in a saucepan and add the sliced onions. Cook them for about 20 minutes on a low heat until they are all nice and soft. Add in the sage leaves and cook for a couple of minutes more, then spread everything out on a plate to cool down.

Then take a sharp knife and carefully slit open the sausages so that you can pop the meat out into a bowl. Add the sage and onion mixture and the breadcrumbs and then get your hands into the bowl and mix it all together. This will either feel really nice or horribly cold and squidgy, depending on whether you like to mess around with meat or not. I do.

Next you need to roll out the puff pastry into a long rectangle about as thick as a pound coin and then cut that rectangle lengthways into two long, thin rectangles. Pick up a handful of the squidgy meat mix and roll it into a long, thin sausage shape. Put it in the middle of one of your rectangles of pastry. Do the same with the other one. Then mix the egg and milk and brush some of this onto the edges of the pastry.

Now for the fun bit! Fold one side of the pastry over the meat so that the filling is wrapped inside and pinch the edges of the pastry to seal it all up. Do the same with the other rectangle of pastry.

Now all you need to do is cut the long rolls into little sausage-roll shapes and arrange them on a baking tray. Brush the rest of the egg and milk mixture over the top to make them nice and shiny in the oven and put them in the oven for about 25 minutes or until they come out all puffed up, sizzling and golden. Serve the first batch hot with a dipping sauce of mustard or tomato ketchup. You will be in heaven.

(Note: my mother steals these during the night when she's hungry. You might wish to invest in a lockable container.)

Chapter Five

I have two days off school because I'm feeling really rough.

Mum isn't too impressed when I drag myself into Karim's shop to do two afternoon shifts, but the thing is I need the ingredients to get practising for when I go to London.

'Oh, goodness me,' says Karim as I lean on a shelf full of bread to get my breath after a coughing fit. 'Little baking girl doesn't sound too good today. Maybe you should take rest.'

I straighten up and get on with stacking shelves.

'Little baking girl is fine,' I say, even though one look at my reflection confirms that I'm not, really. My face is all white and strained-looking and my lips look slightly blue. This lack of oxygen thing is a real nightmare at times. The slightest bit of exertion and I find myself having to sit down for a rest like a sad old lady. Mum's been given a canister of oxygen from the hospital and I plug it in at bedtime. It means that I have plastic tubes put in my nostrils and then the oxygen gets into my body and makes me feel a bit better by morning. But the last thing I want is to have to travel around attached to it, even though Mum has found out that there's a smaller version of the canister which I could carry.

When it's bad, Cystic Fibrosis can be REALLY bad. Some days I struggle to take a proper breath and even to climb the stairs. When it's good, I can almost convince myself that there's nothing wrong with me at all.

Almost.

Karim watches me with concern all afternoon. He's got a hotline straight to my mother's mobile which is really embarrassing, but she insisted on it as a condition of me being allowed in to work.

'I think you should finish early,' he says. 'I still pay you the same, OK?'

I know when I'm beaten. I can hardly stand up straight and all I can think about is getting home and lying on the sofa with a bucket and an inhaler. I take a few sneaky puffs on it now, with my back to Karim. The drugs loosen the tightness in my airways a little and I sigh with relief. One more big cough and I feel slightly better.

'OK,' I say to Karim. 'Thanks. Could I take butter and eggs and white flour today?'

Karim gestures at the shelves of his shop, arms out wide.

'Take whatever you want, little baking girl,' he says. I reckon he still saves money by not paying me an actual wage, so I don't feel too guilty about loading up my bag with several packets of butter. I add some free-range eggs and flour. I'm planning to buy cheese at the special cheese shop in town. Karim does sell cheese but it's hard, square and in packets and tends to be cheddar. I'm looking for something a bit more special, like a nice gruyere, so that I can knock up a fattening batch of cheese straws to put in my school lunch box for the next few days.

That's if I ever get back to school.

The doctors are threatening to keep me in hospital for tests and observation, unless my lung function stabilises over the next few days and Mum is in full agreement with them.

There's less than a month until I am due to attend Britain's Best Teen Baker of the Year.

And there's something else on the horizon.

It's something I try not to think about but every time my lungs get worse it takes a sneaky step closer and looks over my shoulder.

If things don't get better I'm going to have to have a major operation to save my life.

It's called a double lung transplant. It means that I would have somebody else's lungs put into my body and my own diseased ones taken out.

Gross.

When I get home I lie on the sofa and flick the TV on but I can't concentrate.

There's nothing but cookery programmes on and although usually I love watching other people cook and come up with ideas, today I just feel resentful that I'm not in the kitchen whipping up my own recipes.

The thought of standing at the cooker makes me feel exhausted. I stay on the sofa for the rest of the evening and I can't face climbing upstairs to bed, so Mum brings my duvet downstairs and puts it on top of me instead, but even then I can't sleep.

I lie awake watching the moon outside and devising new recipes in my head. Then I just lie there, thinking about my life and where it's going, or not going.

Sometimes people at school ask me what it's like living with an illness that's never going to get any better. I don't mind them asking, because I think that they truly do want to know the answer. It's hard for somebody who is well and has a healthy digestive system and strong, pumping lungs to understand what it's like to not have these things right from the very start of life.

I tell them that I feel the same things as everybody else – happiness, sadness, pain (although maybe more of that than your average kid), excitement, boredom, hunger (on a good day). On a day-to-day basis I guess I pretty much feel the same things in the same way as the other teenagers in my class.

'But what's it like not knowing if you're going to reach adulthood?' some people say. 'What about making plans and stuff? And university.'

I look them in the eye.

'Most of the kids in my class don't have a clue what they want to do when they leave school,' I say. 'And actually, I do know. I want to bake.'

I can see by their doubtful expressions that they don't believe this, but I need to sound strong and positive about everything or else I'd curl up under my duvet and never come out again.

I sigh and sit up. It's obviously going to be one of those nights where thoughts whirl around in my head and stop me from sleeping.

The thought of whirling leads me to think about Viennese whirls. I scribble a few ideas down onto a pad. Classic strawberry jam-filled whirls, I reckon. Made with really good flour and country butter, home-made jam from my cupboard and dusted with icing sugar. Or maybe I might experiment with chocolate whirls instead, sandwiched together with smooth, sweet chocolate buttercream and dipped in hot dark melting chocolate so that half the biscuit is plain and half dipped.

Then I remember my blog. I reach under the sofa and slide out my laptop to log on.

There are another six replies to my first posting!

Five of them are from people offering biscuit recipes. The sixth is from some girl wishing me good luck with the competition.

I scan down the recipes and my mind starts to buzz with chocolate drops and vanilla essence and great luscious big chunks of fudge.

I feel all inspired so I click on the menu bar on my blog

and select 'new post'. Then I tuck my legs up under my duvet and balance the laptop on my knees. This is what I write:

Hi, it's Amelie here – the girl who bakes. Wow – I'm really amazed to come on and find these brilliant biscuit recipes. I promise I will try them all out when I've got the time and energy. That's not supposed to sound wet. The thing is, I kind of suffer from an illness and it saps a lot of my strength. That's why I bake – because I am supposed to try and fatten myself up as much as possible in order to stay alive. Plus I just love baking – it's my favourite thing in life, other than Harry (boyfriend) and my BF Gemma. Anyway, you know I wrote last time about that competition in London? The one I've been selected for? The thing is – I'm too sick to go. Or at least my Mum reckons I am. So I'm drowning not just in mucus (sorry, TMI!) but in disappointment at the moment. But anyway, please carry on sending me your recipes. Any good, sticky cake recipes with a twist would be good. Have any of you ever attempted a chocolate fondant? If not, go and look it up and try to make it. Post a photo online if you can. It's kind of a challenge to get the middle bit runny and not too firm. So I'm signing off now, but I'll post an update of what's happening in my ever-changing life soon. Amelie x

For the first time all week I feel the prick of something resembling appetite.

I lurch up and stagger into the kitchen.

The clank of pans and me banging into cupboards

brings Mum downstairs all prepared to be cross, but when she sees me stirring a pan of rich scrambled eggs and frying up crispy bacon to scatter over the top, she grabs a plate and sits down.

'Ages since I had a midnight snack,' she says. 'It will sit on my hips all night, but who cares?'

She's grinning. I can see that she's relieved that I'm starting to want to eat savoury stuff again. It's usually a good sign.

'Mum?' I say, spooning the creamy eggs onto her plate and sprinkling the salty shreds of bacon on top. I grind black pepper onto my egg before I add the bacon. Then I put a strong pot of tea in the middle of the table and pour full-fat milk into cups. 'If I get better this week, could we talk about London again?'

Mum puts down her fork.

'Amelie,' she says, 'I've discussed this with your father. We really don't think that any time spent in London is going to be any good for your health at all, and your health is our priority.'

I pull a sulky face and shovel in forkfuls of bright yellow egg. The free-range ones are always this sunshine-yellow colour, like the chickens have spent many happy hours pecking about in sun-lit grass. The bacon is a brilliant contrast – sharp, salty and with a nice fatty aftertaste. I've served the bacon and eggs on soft home-made brown bread with loads of butter. Dad says that my cooked breakfasts are the best in the world and I reckon he might just be right.

'Can't we see how I am in a couple of weeks and make a decision then?' I wheedle, pouring Mum a steaming hot cup of tea. 'We don't have to decide now, do we?'

Mum screws her mouth up. I know she finds it really hard to say no to me. I can almost see the two different sides of her head arguing with each other – the one who wants to encourage me to follow my dream versus the one who promised Dad and the doctors to look after me and make sure I didn't get worse.

'Look,' I say, stuffing down more eggs and bacon. 'Appetite back. See? And I feel loads more energetic!'

That's a complete lie. My chest feels heavy and sore and I'm exhausted.

Mum yawns and stands up.

'Well, I don't,' she says. 'It's one o'clock. I suggest we both try and get some sleep. You said you wanted to go back to school in the morning. But I'm sorry – as far as London goes, my decision still has to stay the same.'

My heart sinks towards the blue tiled floor.

'That's right, leave me with all the washing up,' I mutter, but not loud enough for her to hear me. My mess – I need to clear it up. That's one of the many rules in this house.

'I hate you, CF,' I say to my illness as I haul myself up the stairs to reunite with my bed. 'Why do you always have to spoil everything?'

I haven't even done my lung clearing yet.

I take a good snort of my special steroid inhaler to help with lung inflammation and to relieve tightness in my chest. Then I have to do my physio. When I was little Mum had to do the physio on me every single day, whacking me on the back and shoulders and tapping me on the sides in a special way so that all the gunk would come out of my lungs. Now that I'm older I do my own physio by doing special controlled breathing exercises, but I still get a lot of chest infections and I've missed loads of time at school because I can't stop coughing and feeling out of breath.

I do forty minutes of tedious exercises and then I lie in bed feeling sad a while longer and then the next thing I know it's morning and Harry has just texted to say he'll walk me to school if I'm going in.

Harry.

Thank goodness for kind, sweet, handsome romantic Harry.

He's kind of my salvation.

Totally Moreish

Cheese Straws

To make 12, you will need:

A little bit of butter or margarine

100g (3 ½ oz) plain flour

A pinch of salt

A pinch of cayenne pepper or mustard powder

50g (1 ½ oz) butter straight from the fridge, chopped into little bits

1 egg yolk

50g (1 ½ oz) strong cheddar cheese, grated (the larger the flakes of grated cheese, the better)

Some iced water

1 tablespoon of grated parmesan (optional)

A pinch of dried sage or rosemary (optional)

First you need to heat up the oven to 200°C (390°F/gas mark 6). Grease a baking tray with some butter or margarine.

Sieve the flour, cayenne/mustard powder and salt into a bowl. If you're into herbs you could sprinkle in some dried sage or rosemary at this stage too. Add the cubes of butter and rub it all in with your fingertips, until you are left with a bowl of what looks like breadcrumbs.

With a spoon, mix in the egg yolk and the grated cheddar cheese and add a small amount of the iced water (you can chill it in the freezer in a bottle just before you need it). With your hands, knead the mix into a smooth ball of dough. Put this is in some cling film and leave it in the fridge for about 10 or 15 minutes.

Put some flour on a board or work surface and also on your rolling pin. Roll out your dough into a rectangle which is about 4 or 5 millimetres thick. Then get a sharp knife and divide the rectangle into 12 long equal pieces.

Put them on the baking tray and into the hot oven for about 12 minutes until golden and slightly puffed up. You can sprinkle them with Parmesan if you like (I don't) and then put them on a wire rack to cool down. Or you can scoff them straight from the oven, like I do. And be warned – once you've eaten one, you will have to eat another! That's because they are so moreish. IF you manage to resist, you can store them in an airtight tin or jar for a couple of days.

Chapter Six

'Ow,' I say. I rub at the sore area on my chest where you can just see the outline of my portacath beneath the skin. The portacath was put in over a year ago. It lives under my skin on my chest and it makes it easier for the nurses to get treatments into a tube and pumped fast into my body.

I'm at the special CF centre. It's a bit like a hospital, but it's only for people with CF. There's a whole team of people here to help people like me. As I got diagnosed when I was a tiny baby, I've been coming here forever and know everybody in the building. There's Mr Rogers, the consultant who's in charge of my health. Then there's Trisha, the nurse. She does things like pump antibiotics into my portacath when I've got a chest infection and she takes special swab samples from me every few weeks to check that I'm not getting a new infection. People with CF get loads of colds and coughs, same as everybody else, but if I get one it can turn into something nastier and make my lungs even more rubbish than they already are. So if I even get the slightest trace of a sniffle, Mum whips me into the CF centre and gets Trisha to take a sample. If the results come back that I've got an infection, I'm pumped full of extra strong antibiotics, sometimes for many months. Trish also comes to our house if I'm feeling really ill. Mum and Trish are more like friends now, she's been part of our lives for so long.

I also see quite a lot of Diane. She's the dietician who advises me what to eat and when. There's Fiona, the social worker who helps Mum with school issues and tells her how to claim the special allowance she's entitled to for looking after me. And then there's Tom, the physiotherapist. He taught Mum how to treat me at home with her hands to help loosen all the stubborn mucus in my chest. Two years ago he taught me how to do something called autogenic drainage which I can do on my own at home so that Mum doesn't need to get so involved with my physio any more. For this I have to lie on my back on my bed and do three special sorts of breathing: unsticking, collecting and evacuating the mucus out of my battered lungs. The noises I make while I am doing it are not pretty. I'm supposed to do it twice a day but I always fall out with Mum because I tend to, erm, forget. Or life gets in the way. Or I don't really want Gemma coming round in the middle of it, even though she's really good about the whole CF thing.

Or worst of all, I might have a batch of muffins to take out of the oven.

Flour Power!

So I'm at hospital having my portacath flushed through. I have to have this done every month to make sure that it doesn't get clogged or else my antibiotics can't get into my system. It feels a bit uncomfortable but the main issue is that I just get so bored waiting for it all to be finished.

I'm in a room of my own. People with CF have to be very careful not to infect one another. That sucks. It's bad enough being in hospital so often without being able to speak to people your own age who might just understand what you're going through.

I've got a pile of food magazines on my lap and I'm leafing through the latest recipes by Jamie, Nigella and Gordon, whilst trying not to notice what's going on in my chest.

'She's been more poorly this month than she's been for years,' Mum is saying to the consultant who's just come into the room. I've known Mr Rogers for years, ever since I was about six. I still don't really understand why the consultants here are called 'Mr' and not 'Doctor' even though they ARE doctors, but I've got used to it now.

'Hi, Mr R,' I say, flicking the glossy pages of a BBC food magazine. 'How's it hanging?'

Mum sighs.

'Not a great question to ask a doctor,' says Mr Rogers. 'I'm likely to give you a long, medical and potentially boring answer.'

I smile. I like Mr Rogers and his weird sense of humour. Somehow he always manages to make me feel like Amelie-The-Person rather than just Amelie-The-Patient.

'Your Mum tells me you want to go to London,' he says. 'Some big competition, I hear. That does sound very exciting.'

'Yeah,' I say, 'but has she also told you she's not allowing me to go?'

Mum flushes pale pink when I say that. Her face clashes with her red jacket. I think of the pink slices from a tub of Neapolitan ice cream and the red of the strawberry sauce I like to pour over them.

'I was just about to get round to that,' she says, all defensive and huffy. 'Mr Rogers is a very busy man.'

He perches on the edge of the bed where I'm lying.

'Not too busy to discuss your health,' he says. 'So I take it you still want to go to London?'

I put down the magazines with a sigh. I've just found a glorious twist on a traditional baked cheesecake recipe which involves major use of chocolate.

'Of course I do,' I say. 'It's only like the biggest baking competition in the country. And I don't see why I can't still go, so long as I'm careful and look after myself.'

Mum stands up and folds her arm. She looks tired, wary and wired up all at the same time.

'I'm getting a bit fed up of this stuck record,' she says in a voice I hardly ever hear. 'I've told you you're not going, and that's that. Don't try to swing me by dragging Mr Rogers into it all.'

Mr Rogers stands up and clears his throat.

'It's your annual review next week, isn't it?' he says. 'Perhaps if I might suggest, Mrs Day, we could make a final decision based upon the results of that?'

Mum flushes again. I can tell that she's angry that Mr Rogers hasn't entirely backed her up.

'Oh, alright,' she says. 'But I can't see Amelie being much better than she is now and right now she is in no fit state to go anywhere. I'll be at the coffee machine.'

She goes out of the room and lets the door bang behind her.

Mr Rogers and I regard one another for a moment. He has kind eyes – dark like chocolate raisins and with a sort of glint behind them. I try to picture what his kids are like and reckon that he's a good father.

'I only want to get on with my life,' I say in a whisper. 'That's all.'

Mr Rogers nods and puts his hand on my shoulder for a moment. The brief gesture causes tears to well up in my eyes.

'I'll leave you in the capable hands of Sister,' he says. The nurse is unhooking the flush from my portacath. 'Don't worry. I'm sure we can sort something out.'

My heart lifts a little.

'Oh, here,' I call after his retreating back. 'I made you something.'

Mr Rogers comes back and peels back the lid of the box I'm holding out.

'I did them all on a medical theme,' I say, shy.

He bursts out laughing. I've been practising biscuits for the competition. Inside are some iced golden syrup cookies with little piped pictures on top. I've done a pair of lungs on one, a heart on another and a selection of pills, beds, syringes and stethoscopes on the rest. It took me half the night to perfect the drawings and I did them in a dark green colour in the same shade as Mr Roger's operating overalls.

'You are something else, Amelie,' he says, wiping his eyes. 'I can't eat these. They're too good. But of course, I will.'

Then he leaves me, still laughing to himself. I let the nurse clean me up and prepare me for going home.

Dad calls round to see me after I get home from hospital.

I'm in the kitchen making mini carrot cakes with buttercream frosting. I've cut some carrot shapes out of my leftover fondant icing and coloured them orange and I'm just sticking these on top of the finished cakes. There's a pile of homework upstairs with my name on it, but after a day spent in the hot, disinfectant-smelling air of the hospital, I fancied letting my creative vision run riot so I've ditched the idea of doing maths until later.

'There,' I say, standing back to admire my handiwork. The little square cakes stand to attention in neat lines on the rack, each one covered in fluffy buttercream which I've run a fork through to make peaks that look a bit like snowdrifts.

'Oh yes!' says Dad, heading towards the rack with a

purposeful look in his eye. 'I reckon you need a second opinion on those from your Chief Taster.'

I sigh.

'Harry is Chief Taster,' I say. 'You can be Back-up Taster, if you like.'

Dad frowns.

'I've been relegated to the sidelines,' he says. 'Wow. And I'm your favourite Dad and all that.'

I let him pick out a cake and bite into the rich sponge.

'Good?' I say. 'I added some lemon juice just to make it a bit different.'

'Mm,' says Dad with his cheeks bulging. 'Excellent. And I would love to see what you can do with a courgette.'

I smile and click the kettle on. Mum comes downstairs and gives Dad a peck on the cheek.

'Thought I heard you,' she says. 'Why don't you come outside and admire my petunias?'

'Oh, right,' says Dad. 'How much more excitement can one man take?'

He winks at me and then heads off outside with Mum and they walk around our back courtyard garden, staring into pots and tubs and chatting avidly all the time.

I make the tea and bang on the window and they wave but don't come in.

I'm about to bang again and then I realise what they're doing. Why Dad has come over, in fact. They're discussing the London question. They're talking about me.

For a moment I feel a surge of anger. Then I bite it down again. I know it's only because they care. But if they're discussing something about my future, then really I should be out there taking part in the discussion with them.

I put the three mugs on a tray and add three of my mini carrot cakes and I head out the back. Mum and Dad have stopped looking at plants. Mum is now facing Dad with her hands on her hips which can't be a good thing, as that's the position she adopts when she's telling me off about something. Dad is staring at his feet and shuffling them about which is also not good.

I sigh and offer the tray.

'I know you're talking about me,' I say. 'Which is why I've come out here. Plus I can't actually lip-read through the window which is kind of annoying.'

Dad smiles when I say this. Mum doesn't.

'Sometimes your father and I need to talk about stuff in private,' she says. 'You could have given us another minute, surely?'

I look at Dad. He shrugs and reaches for a mug of tea.

'Your mother's in charge here,' he says. 'What she says, goes.'

He says this in a mechanical way, like he's rehearsed it. I look at him more closely. He doesn't look very pleased. I'm not sure whether he's annoyed with Mum or with me for coming outside and interrupting.

'Dad,' I say. 'What do YOU think about me going to London? Honestly?'

Dad glances at Mum. She gives him an imploring sort of look, like she's trying to affect what he's about to say, but Dad sits down on the edge of a tub full of pink begonias and takes a gulp of his tea.

'Honestly?' he says. 'I think it's a cracking idea.'

'John!' says my mother in a shocked tone of voice. 'I thought we just agreed?'

Dad rubs his eyes and blinks.

'I didn't agree anything,' he says. 'You told me not to say something, but Mel has asked me a direct question and I'm going to give her a direct answer.'

I look at my Dad with new eyes full of respect, love and a bit of fear. Does he know that disagreeing with Mum can be like throwing a lit match into a room full of petrol? Oh yeah – he does. That's why they got divorced.

'Oh, Gordon Bennett,' says Mum. She often mentions Gordon. Neither of us has ever worked out exactly who he is. 'Thanks a bunch. You've just made my next few weeks a hell of a lot harder.'

She looks really upset, like she's going to cry. I get up and offer her the cake plate.

'Cake is not the answer to everything,' she snaps. Then she looks at the tiny orange carrots with their green stems and relents. 'Oh go on then – just one.'

She eats it with an angry look on her face.

'For what it's worth,' says Dad. 'I happen to think that Mel doing this competition is a fantastic idea. Our beautiful, talented and creative daughter has been offered an exciting opportunity which she'd be a fool to pass up on. Surely this is what her life should be like? Shouldn't we be supporting this? Don't you remember what the counsellor at the CF centre said?'

I remember full well what the counsellor said, because I was there too and it was the first thing that anybody at the centre had ever said to me that made perfect, total sense.

The counsellor said that, now I was in my teens, Mum ought to stop acting so much like 'the CF Police.' They meant that she was trying too hard to control what I did because she was so anxious about my health. The counsellor reckoned that stopping me doing things I really wanted to do was having a far worse effect on me than just skipping a treatment or forgetting to take a pill.

Mum gets a folding chair out of the shed and sits down with a sigh.

'Of course I remember,' she says. 'I love the fact that Amelie has got through to the quarter-finals. I'm as excited by that bit as you are, John. But the fact remains that a week in Central London is going to be detrimental to her overall health. And isn't THAT our main concern? Damn, this carrot cake is good!'

I allow myself a small, victorious smile at that.

Mum locks eyes with my dad and they have a kind of stare-off, like the black cat and the Siamese who are always passing through our garden in a flurry of teeth, eyes, yowls and spits.

In the end Dad gets up and puts his cup and plate back on the tray.

'I don't think we're going to agree, are we?' he says. 'You're more concerned with her physical health and I'm concerned with the mental. How do we meet in the middle?'

Mum shakes her head.

'We don't,' she says in a tired voice. 'I'm the one who lives with her. So I will make the decision. OK?'

Dad nods, but his face looks sad. It mirrors my own. I can see my fabulous baking opportunity slipping even further into the great mixing bowl of life, to be lost in a mess of eggs, flour and butter.

He gets up and walks back over to the cobbles and out of the garden gate towards his car.

'See you, kiddo,' he says, blowing me a kiss.

He blows one to Mum, as well but she pretends not to see.

Wow. Parents can be so stressful. I feel worn out from witnessing their conversation and I have to have another fortifying carrot cake and cup of tea.

'I guess that's it then,' I say to Mum as we tidy up in the kitchen. 'I should forget about going to London.'

My voice must sound sad because Mum comes over and gives me a hug.

'I don't think you can go, love,' she says. 'But if you like, we'll get your annual review over with and make a final decision. OK?'

That's definitely progress. I give her a hug back and offer to cook supper which for me is like the biggest treat out there.

'Can I invite Harry over for dinner?' I say.

Mum smiles.

'OK,' she says.

I watch her back disappearing upstairs and I realise

that she's still got no intention of letting me go to London. The annual review is hardly ever good news. My lung function is always less good than the year before. I can feel it. I get more out of breath than I used to and my coughing has taken on a new and deadly rattle. I'm dreading the bit where the doctors work out my BMI too. That stands for 'Body Mass Index' and it works out whether I'm the right weight for my height. I've never once been the right amount and the nutritionist always tells me that I need to pack in more calories.

I sink down onto the stairs and bury my face in my arms.

I've got to get to London.

I've just got to.

The rest of my life depends on it.

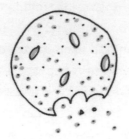

Golden Syrup Cookies

To make between 20-24 of these delicious crunchy cookies, you will need:

455g (16oz) self-raising flour

230g (8oz) butter

230g (8oz) sugar (half white caster, half brown — for the brown sugar, I use Muscovado or Demerara, but any brown sugar will do)

120ml (4oz) golden syrup

Anything you would like to add to the biscuit mix — peanuts, chocolate chips, even Smarties!

Heat the oven to 180°C/360°F/gas mark 4.

First of all you need to melt the butter in a pan (don't boil, just simmer on a low heat). Then add in the golden syrup until it's all melted into a nice gloopy liquid.

In a mixing bowl, sieve your flour, add the sugar and mix this together, then pour in the butter and syrup mix. Give it all a good stir until you've got a fairly stiff biscuit dough.

At this point you can add in anything you want to go inside your cookies. My favourite is peanuts, even salted ones – for some reason the salt and the cookies go very well together.

Shape the mixture into balls just bigger than a golf ball and place them on a couple of greased baking trays. You will need to leave quite a lot of space around each biscuit because when they cook they blow up much bigger and could end up joined to the next biscuit! Probably best to limit the numbers to 10 biscuits per baking tray. If you've got any dough left over, refrigerate it and roll it out to make more cookies in a day or two.

Bake them in the oven for about 15 minutes or until they are golden and firm to the touch. Let them cool on the wire rack and then store in an airtight tin.

If you want, at the stage where you mix the flour with the sugar, you could swap 50g (1 ½ oz) of the flour for 50g of chocolate powder for a more chocolaty biscuit – yum – or even 50g of desiccated coconut for a different flavour. These biscuits are a pretty good way of experimenting with loads of different flavours and toppings.

Chapter Seven

I miss five days at school.

Trish's latest sample shows that I have another chest infection brewing and I need to take more antibiotics in addition to the ones I take every day by inhaling from my nebuliser. Mum's been shown how to feed the new stronger drugs into a tube that feeds in through my portacath, so she does this every day and I lie on the sofa and complain about not being able to make cakes. I read recipe books instead, one after another, and start scribbling down pages of ideas.

I glance at the list of rules from the competition organisers. For the two baked desserts, I have to make some mini-puddings and then a larger one. I'm agonising between dark chocolate fondant mini-cakes with Chantilly crème or rich moist mini-Bakewell tarts with home-made almond ice cream. For the larger cake I'm pretty sure I'm going to do my famous sticky German gingerbread with vanilla custard.

So I wait until the fourth day when I've started to feel a bit better and I go back into the kitchen and start messing around with flour and sugar and peanuts and eggs. Mum comes in from work and does a big blissed-out sniff of the air and tries not to look at the smeared work surfaces, the flour all over the floor and the knives covered in butter and flung into bowls.

'I hope you're not overdoing it,' Mum says.

I pull a face. We're only just speaking, Mum and I. We have a pretty intense relationship at the best of times. She's the only one who sees me when I'm really sick and she's the one who has to deal with it. Sometimes I don't even want to look at her worried, tired face any more because all it does is remind me how sick I get.

The day before yesterday she tried to put her arm around me while she held a bowl in front of my face for me to cough stuff into and I pushed her away. Hard. The bowl fell to the floor and Mum jumped as if she'd been shot, but then she saw my face and chest contorting with the effort of getting all the mucus up and her face softened. She sat next to me on the edge of the bed, taking care not to touch me that time, and she held the bowl until I'd finished and carried it out and cleaned it in the bathroom. Then she got me a glass of water and for supper she made me a bowl of thick mushroom soup with a swirl of cream on the top.

'You need to eat it,' she said. 'You're getting too thin again.'

I still felt sick but I drank the soup and a faint colour crept back into my white face.

Mum is brilliant. And I know she is, which makes it feel really horrid when I'm mean to her and yell stuff at her.

Sometimes I tell her to get the hell out of my bedroom.

It's two days until my annual review.

I'm back at school for a half-day because I'm tiring really easily at the moment and Mum wants me home straight after lunch. It's kind of tough dipping in and out of school like this. I feel I miss out on a lot of stuff, even just the classroom gossip. The other kids are fine about it and some of them make a point of asking me how I am, but I still feel like I stick out like a sore lung.

It doesn't help that I'm smaller and thinner than most of the rest of my class. Despite that, I'm a pretty key member of the football team. Because I'm small and wiry I can dodge the other players and hold onto the ball.

I play a match in the morning after using my inhaler and then I sit through double maths and by the time the bell goes for lunch I feel pretty wiped. I don't tell anybody. There are teachers who look out for me and if I told them I was feeling bad they'd send me to the school nurse and she'd ring Mum straight away.

'You OK?' Harry says. We're walking towards the back of the school to eat our lunch underneath the big oak tree near the playing fields and the short walk feels like miles to me. Harry's not in my class but in the year above. We only eat lunch together twice a week for half an hour because he does tennis club and judo club during lunch break on Tuesdays and Thursdays and I do art club on Friday lunchtimes, so it's kind of special being able to sit underneath the tree with him.

'Yeah. Ish,' I say, sitting down on the damp grass and leaning back against the trunk with a sigh. I'm more honest with Harry than I am with anybody else on the planet, even Gemma. There's something about Harry which means I'm more patient with him than anyone else in my life, too. I think it's because he's quite casual and normal about the whole CF thing. That doesn't mean he's uncaring. He does keep a keen eye on me. Just that he is the opposite of 'The CF Police.' He lets me express opinions and do things I want to do without warning me all the time that whatever it is will make my CF worse.

I lean back against the tree. Then a fit of coughing takes hold of me and I lean forwards and cough and retch and make revolting rattling noises from my chest until I'm aching with tiredness.

'Sorry,' I whisper. 'I hate this cough sometimes.'

Harry nods. Then he snaps open his lunchbox and reveals loads of healthy stuff like apples and bits of green salad. He knows full well that he's going to get half my cake and chocolate supply, so this is not as worthy as it might seem.

'Swap?' he says, holding out a tub of cucumber and tomato and eyeing up the lemon muffins that I made last night. They're drizzled with icing made with fresh lemons and there's a sharp lemon syrup running through the sponge of each little cake so that biting into them is all zingy and surprising and makes the insides of your cheeks go a bit funny.

'Ha, ha,' I say. I take one piece of cucumber and pass the rest of the salad back to him. I can't eat tomatoes because my stomach already makes too much acid and they just make it worse. Then I give him one of the muffins and keep two back for myself. I'm not being greedy – I just need to cram in the calories or else I'll get even thinner.

'So,' says Harry, not looking me in the eye but frowning over at the science lab as if he's waiting for something to explode out of the roof. 'Are you feeling really rough today?'

I sigh and put the cake box down on my lap. I finish chewing and make a mental note to add slightly less sugar to the lemon syrup next time, then I rest my head on his warm shoulder.

'Oh, I dunno,' I say, sniffing the starchy smell of his white school shirt. Harry's mother is very keen on fragrant fabric conditioners with pictures of tulips on the bottle. 'Kind of. Better than I did three days ago. But I'm dreading the annual review.'

Harry rests his cheek on the top of my head for a moment and then bites into his apple. He takes such huge bites that half the apple disappears into his mouth right away.

'Have you had your thingy?' he says. He's looking at my schoolbag.

I pull a face.

'You sound like Mum,' I say. 'Except she would refer to it by its correct name.'

Harry laughs.

'OK then – have you had your Creon?' he says, passing me the school bag. 'Trust you to take something that sounds like a character from *Star Trek*.'

I get out my plastic box of pills and take a few of the enzymes that I have to take with every meal. I gulp down some water and then lean back and look up at the clouds drifting over the sky.

'Harry,' I say. My voice sounds clogged. I reach into the bag and pull out my inhaler, take a few deep breaths on it. Better. 'Where do you think we go when we die?'

Harry gives me a startled look when I say that. He tries to cover it straight up by leaning forwards and fiddling with the laces on his trainers, but I saw his face lose the smiley look for a moment and a tiny, mean part of me feels pleased that I actually mean that much to him.

'Dunno,' he says. 'Not sure we really go anywhere. Why? Do you want to go somewhere else?'

I shiver and pull the sleeves of my cardigan down. It's cooling down out here and loads of kids are heading back inside because the bell's going to go any minute. I'm one of the few kids who don't rush anywhere at school and I'm often slightly late for lessons. It's not because I'm trying to be a rebel or anything cool like that. It's because if I rush,

I get out of breath and enter the classroom doubled up coughing and let's face it, I might as well have a red light flashing on and off on my head and a sign saying 'SICK PERSON' in big letters around my neck if my cough starts up in the classroom. Once I'm coughing, classes come to a halt. I don't think that the teachers can hear themselves talk over the racket.

You might think that a person with CF would want to rush more, because they know that their life is likely to be a whole load shorter than everybody else's, but I'm not really like that, even though sometimes I'm keen to pack as many experiences into my life as possible.

When I watch the rest of my class rush about I kind of sink back and take a deep breath and let them get on with it. It's like I already know what life's about and this urgent rush to get everywhere seems a bit stupid. I mean – I know that life is short and goes fast, even for people who live to be eighty. So sometimes I like to lean back and take stock of things and notice them properly. After all, I don't have so much time left to notice things, do I?

'I've just been thinking about it loads,' I say. 'Sorry. I didn't mean to be all gruesome and morbid. Kind of stupid, huh?'

I turn to look at Harry with a grin on my face but for once he doesn't return it.

Instead he kicks at the wall outside the door into the main school corridor. When he turns to me his face is red and ugly.

'Mel,' he says, 'you're thirteen. Yeah, I know you have

a life-threatening illness. I know that and I accept it. But all this crap about life after death is doing my head in, alright? Maybe I don't want to think about you not being around, yeah? Did you ever try to look at this from *my* point of view?'

He flings open the double doors to the school hall so hard that they bang against the walls and slam back, nearly injuring a couple of girls from my class.

'Sorry,' I say to the girls. They scowl at me and raise their eyes at one another. I wouldn't blame them if they were thinking there goes the pathetic sick girl who can't get anything right.

Tears threaten to spill out of my eyes so I fumble in my pocket for a Mars Bar and shove it savagely into my mouth.

I go into the girl's cloakroom and sit on a bench. I cough until my eyes are watering yet again.

Then I lean against the wall with my eyes closed and wish I was somebody else.

Chapter Eight

Sometimes I dream up recipes in the night.

I keep a pen and pad by the bed just in case I get any brilliant ideas. The cakes I invent in my sleep are often loads more colourful and unusual than the ones I cook up when I'm awake.

Gemma's always telling me that she dreams about boys off *The X Factor* or else she dreams that she's not finished her homework and the teacher is yelling at her.

I reckon those dreams are a bit dull.

I dream about lavender icing and white chocolate chips. I dream of caramel sauce being poured from an enormous jug onto a giant treacle sponge. I dream of great vats of whipped cream and enormous sacks of coloured hundreds-and-thousands pouring out over my head and raining down on my body. I once dreamed that I was being chased through a field by a giant brown cupcake with stick legs and big waving hands but I'm not sure what that meant.

Anyway, it's a safe bet that most nights when I close my eyes, some sort of cake is going to make a feature in my dreams.

I never, ever dream about my illness. I guess I live so much of it during the day that my subconscious doesn't really need to explore it during the night. That's why I like being asleep so much. When I'm asleep, it's like the CF doesn't exist.

The night before my annual review it takes me hours to get to sleep.

When I finally drift off, exhausted, in the early hours, I don't dream at all.

That scares me more than any nightmare I might have had.

It's like being dead.

Mum insists we have a good breakfast even though my insides are really sore and my stomach is churning and making weird noises.

'It's a very long day for you today, Amelie,' she says. 'You need some energy.'

I give a feeble snort. I can barely sit up straight at the table after my bad night. I can't help thinking back to my last annual review when I went for a run round the block before we headed off to the CF centre and spent the whole day bouncing off the clinic walls with frustration, desperate to get home and bake.

Today I almost feel like it would be a relief to spend some time lying around in hospital doing not-very-much. I haven't spoken to Harry since he got angry two days ago and he hasn't texted me which is well out of character. Gemma reckons that boys need to go off and have sulking time on their own and that he'll come out of his cave when he's ready, but I'm not so sure.

I hate not speaking to Harry. It's like the rug has been pulled out from under my feet. He's my support system. He even offered to come with me to all my medical appointments, but I've never let him. I reckon it's bad enough Mum seeing me at my worst without Harry having to see it as well. Something about tall, fresh-faced, glowing athletic Harry looks all wrong against the clinical whiteness of the sterile hospital rooms where I spend so much of my time.

'Take it off the heat,' I say to Mum. She's attempting to make scrambled egg but she's never quite got the technique right, leaving it on the gas for too long so that it always turns out dry and rubbery and split into hundreds of little bits. I like my scrambled eggs soft, yellow and creamy and to get that result you have to take the pan away from the heat before they've finished cooking.

'I don't want you to get Salmonella,' says Mum, but she starts spooning the egg onto some of my home-made granary bread. She puts two plates in front of us and pours me a cup of tea from our brown pot.

'Stewed,' I say in an automatic way, staring at the orangey scum floating on top of my cup.

Mum ignores me. She's used to me making a fuss about the way everything is done in the kitchen.

She's got the day off work today and is dressed in leggings and a floaty top instead of her usual smart business suit and heels. Even though she's quite old, she manages somehow to look trendy. If some of the other mothers of kids at school wore leggings, they'd look tragic.

I can tell that she's really worried. I can hear it in her over-bright voice and see it in the way she keeps staring up at the clock.

She's come on every single one of my annual reviews and seen how things have started to slide downwards a little bit more every year. Dad comes to them whenever he can take time away from work, too. If he can't make it, Mum rings him at the end of the day and they discuss my results over the phone.

I sigh as I force down the scrambled egg into my sore guts.

'Creon,' says Mum. She pushes my pill box across the table. I take a few of the capsules and gulp them down with the stewed tea.

'Aspirin,' she says next. I glance up, surprised.

'I don't take aspirin,' I say. 'Do I?'

I take so many tablets I'm not always sure what they all are.

Mum smiles.

'The aspirin are for me,' she says. 'I always get a headache at the hospital. It's the stress of waiting about in those stuffy rooms.'

She slips a yellow box into her handbag and stands up.

'Right,' she says. 'Let's go and get this over with and then we can come back home.'

We're at the CF centre by 8.30. I've got several different staff to see over the course of the day and numerous tests. They reckon I'll be at the hospital until the early evening, so Mum has packed up a huge bag full of high-calorie drinks, snacks and tablets to keep me going. Plus she's got my inhaler, my nebuliser and a box of plasters in case the skin around my portacath snags and bleeds.

The first thing I'm having done is a series of blood tests to make sure that I'm not getting liver disease or anything else that affects my organs. We sit in a grey waiting room with loads of bored-looking people and wait for nearly half an hour to get called in. I roll up my sleeve and let the nurse extract my dark blood into a series of little tubes. It comes out cherry-red and glossy, which gets me thinking about red cherry icing on cupcakes and I get so excited about this new icing I've not yet tried that I don't even hear what the nurse is saying to me and have to be nudged by Mum. I press the gauze into the hole in my arm and she puts a plaster over the top.

That's the easy bit done.

The next thing I have to have done is a CT scan. This is so that the doctors can see my lungs and whether my airways have been damaged by repeated chest infections. I only usually get this once at year at the annual review.

I have to lie inside a tunnel for the scan. When I first had this done I got really panicky at being in the dark, enclosed space, but I've had so many of them now that I don't even register it. When it's done the radiographer lets me take a look on a computer screen. Not everybody gets to see their x-rays straight away, but I know all the staff in this place so I'm allowed to.

'Hmm,' I say, staring at my ribs on the picture. My portacath is visible too, a tiny circle at the top of my chest. 'I look like a rack of lamb.'

Mum laughs.

'She translates everything into food terms,' she says to the radiographer. 'It's her way of coping.'

I give Mum an angry look.

'No it's not,' I hiss. 'I just think I look like meat ribs, that's all.'

In fact I'm trying not to look at the strange inflated shape of my chest on the x-ray. I know full well that this is not good. As if she's sensing my despair, the radiographer switches off her machine and my ribs disappear from view.

A man in a green overall comes in and puts me in a wheelchair to take me up to the physio department.

'I can walk, you know!' I protest, but deep down I'm relieved to be pushed. The CF centre has loads of long, shiny grey corridors and the x-ray department is miles from all the other offices. I'm out of breath already today. I'm not sure whether it's because I'm nervous, or because I didn't sleep, but my energy levels feel as if they might be hitting an all-time low.

Great.

Tom comes to greet me in the physio department with his usual wide, white smile.

'Hi Mel,' he says. 'How's it going?'

I don't think he really expects an answer to this because he's turned his back to me and is leading us through to his office, but I give a weak smile and allow the hospital orderly to help me out of my chair.

Tom makes me lie on the couch and show him how I'm doing my autogenic drainage. I demonstrate my brilliant breathing techniques and Mum tries not to wince at the ghastly sound of my rattling mucus clearing from my airways.

'OK,' he says afterwards. 'Are you still on twice a day?'

I nod. Mum gives me a harsh look until I'm forced to look down at my feet.

'I might forget sometimes,' I mumble. 'Lots of homework, you know.'

Tom smiles, but underneath the smile is a look of concern.

'I think you need to really make sure you do it, Mel,' he says. 'And I haven't seen your x-ray results yet, but by the sounds of it we need to increase the number of times you do the breathing to at least three times a day.'

I groan and bury my head on the desk for a moment.

When I come up I go dizzy for a moment and clutch at the sides of my chair.

I can see Mum trying not to have a panic.

'I'm fine,' I say. I sit up straight and force a smile back on. 'OK. I'll do it three times a day. Promise.'

Mum and Tom exchange a few more ideas and concerns while I sit there all bored, staring at the leaflet stand in his office and trying to make cake words out of 'Cystic Fibrosis'. I'm still struggling with that when Mum drags me off for my next two appointments.

I'm kind of dreading these ones.

The first is with the nutritionist, Diane.

She's the cleanest woman in the world. Her white coat is spotless and her shiny brown hair is tied back into a neat knot. Her glasses sparkle and her shoes are highly polished. Her office is very bare and tidy, with two identical pot plants placed one at each end of the windowsill. I reckon if Diane passed through our kitchen at home after I'd made a cheesecake, she might well have a heart attack from the shock of the mess.

'OK,' she says, sitting behind her desk and gesturing at me and Mum to sit down. 'I can see that you've lost just a little bit of weight, Amelie, since you last came in.'

I last came in for weighing about four months ago so this is not such good news.

Diane weighs me on her digital scales and then measures my height. She calculates my Body Mass Index, dividing my weight by my height.

'You're quite a lot less than you should be,' she says. 'Have you been getting your maximum calories in every day?'

I nod. This at least is true. Mum can't pick me up on this one. I've been stuffing my face with cake, chocolate and crisps on top of normal meals for what feels like forever.

'Hmm,' says Diane. 'I'm going to suggest something to help with your weight, but I don't want you to panic, OK?'

Why is it that as soon as somebody medical says the words 'don't panic,' you immediately want to scream and panic and thrash about?

I feel cold and thin. The weight of whatever she's about to suggest is already hovering over my head, about to plunge down and change my life yet again. I glance at Mum. She's gripping her hands together so hard that they have turned white and she's fiddling with the finger where her wedding ring used to be, except of course it's not there any longer.

'It's alright,' says Diane. 'Loads of people with CF have this. I'm going to suggest that you're set up with a feeding tube at home to pump calories into you overnight while you sleep. It really won't affect you when you're awake at all.'

I blow out my lips in despair, forgetting that I can't breathe that well as it is. The short dip in oxygen leaves me coughing my guts up for nearly five minutes. Diane gets a grey cardboard bowl and holds it under my mouth while Mum hovers about chewing her lip and looking agonised.

When I've finished I sit up again, exhausted.

'Sorry,' I say. 'You were talking about the tube. How would it go into my body?'

'Through your stomach via a gastrostomy,' says Diane. 'You'd have to have that put in under general anaesthetic. Then it would just stay in your stomach, closed off by a button during the day. It would be easy for you or Mum to connect the tube at night-time. We can get about 2000 more calories into you while you're sleeping.'

I nod. It's amazing the things I've had to get used to over the years. Guess one more tube isn't going to make so much difference. I still feel scared about it though. Not so much about the tube, but what it means about the general direction my health is heading in.

Diane gets me to fill in some forms saying that I'd like to be admitted to day surgery to have the gastrostomy fitted and then Mum helps me walk to the next appointment because I'm feeling tired and wobbly.

'Poor old you,' she says, squeezing my arm as we walk along. 'Bet you can't wait to get home. I think we'll get a DVD out tonight and maybe have fish and chips. OK?'

I know she's trying to be kind and cheer me up and all that, but it's not really working. All I can think about is the competition in two weeks' time and the fact that I've hardly done any preparation for it and all I can see up ahead of me is a huge black mountain blocking my way to London. Of course being me, the mountain is made out of thousands of black olives all gleaming and glistening with oil and dotted with chilli and garlic, but even this dramatic image fails to cheer me up much.

We've reached the office next door to Mr Rogers, my consultant, now. Trish is already there. She's going to do my lung function test and then Mum and I are going to have a late lunch and then wait a couple of hours while Mr Rogers gets all my results together and gives me his opinion on them.

The lung function test is the thing I dread most of all. It's really simple. All I have to do is blow hard into a machine and it measures the volume of air blown out of my lungs. Trish then compares this number to the number she recorded when I last did the test and then she can tell if my lung function has got better or worse.

I breathe as hard as I can into her machine and as usual it leaves me coughing and breathless again, so we go through the whole process of Trish holding a bowl under my mouth and Mum pacing up and down. Then Trish gestures for me to sit down.

I can see by her sympathetic face that it's not great news.

'Yes, you've guessed it,' she says. 'Your lung function is down a fair bit since last year's review. It's only at forty-eight per cent as opposed to last time when you were at nearly sixty. We'll get the x-ray results and then Mr Rogers will be able to talk to you about what we might be able to do next. OK?'

Trish is really nice so I give her a big smile, even though my heart is aching at the news and I can't even look at Mum.

'You should get some better sweets for CF patients,' I say, pointing to the tired pile of fruit lollies that she keeps to give the little kids. 'There aren't enough calories in those. You should be handing out fudge made with condensed milk. I'll knock some up for you next time.'

Trish laughs.

'Fair point,' she says. 'See you later.'

Then we stagger off downstairs to find the canteen.

The canteen in the CF centre does hot meals and sandwiches and sells loads of high calorie junk food as well so Mum piles up my tray with Shepherd's Pie, roast potatoes and green beans and adds a strawberry milkshake and a piece of sponge cake.

She chooses a ham salad for herself.

'I think I'd rather have yours,' I say, eyeing up the small meal with envy. My guts feel like they're twisted in knots and I've got a faint sick feeling, not helped by the strong smell of hospital disinfectant all over the place.

'Tough,' says Mum. 'You heard what Diane said. You're losing way too much weight. So you need to eat this.'

Mum is going into 'CF Police' mode again, but I'm too tired to argue. I pick up the fork and examine the mixture of meat and mashed potato I'm about to put into my mouth.

'Packet gravy,' I say, all doleful. When I make Shepherd's Pie I do amazing gravy with fresh sage, home-made lamb stock and a dash of Mum's favourite red wine when she's not looking. 'And cheap white potatoes, not Maris Piper. Yuk.'

Mum sighs.

'Oh Amelie,' she says. 'You are funny. Only you could be complaining about the gravy when you've just been given all that difficult news to digest. Most kids don't care what potatoes they're eating so long as they're made into chips.'

I prod at my over-salted meal and consider this.

'Mother,' I say. 'You of all people should know by now that I am not Most Kids.'

Mum gives me a look that I find hard to read for a moment and then I realise that she can't speak because if she did, she'd start to cry.

I give her a weak smile and we eat the rest of our lunch in silence.

After another two hours of hanging about drinking endless cups of tea and coffee and high-calorie milkshakes, Mr Rogers finally comes out of his office and calls us in.

'Sorry you've had such a long wait,' he says. 'I've had to wait for the various results to come in from other departments. We want to make sure that we've got all the information before we talk to you.'

He ushers us into his office. Because he's a senior consultant he's got posh furniture and much larger pot plants than everybody else. I sink down into the soft, expensive leather armchair and Mum takes the one next to me.

'OK, hit me with it,' I say, before Mr Rogers can start trying to dress up whatever he's about to say with lots of medical speak. 'I've got some cake tins waiting for action at home.'

Mr Rogers twinkles at me with his kind eyes over the top of his glasses and then returns his attention to the files on his desk.

'The usual evidence of mild liver disease,' he says. 'Nothing to worry about at this stage. And all the other blood tests came back fine. But your lung function tests are down on last time and your loss of weight is quite marked. I gather Diane has spoken to you about gastrostomy. Any questions you might have about that?'

I shake my head. I've got a leaflet about it in my bag and I kind of understand the idea behind it.

'What about my lungs?' I say. 'Do I need to do even more extra physio? Tom said three times a day would be enough.'

Mr Rogers exchanges a quick look with Mum. Then he clicks on a machine next to his desk and holds up my chest x-ray so that I can see it lit up again.

He points to an area of criss-cross lines in front of my ribs.

'See these?' he says. 'Because you've had chronic infection in your airways, they're now full of infected mucus and there's air trapped in your lungs, which is why your chest looks expanded. The long word for this is "bronchiectasis". The worse it gets, the more trouble your lungs will have clearing carbon dioxide from your bloodstream.'

'Wow,' I say. 'Another long word for my collection. Cheers, Doc.'

Mum flinches at my casual way of addressing Mr Rogers.

'How do we stop it getting worse?' she says. 'Is it a question of more physio?'

Mr Rogers takes off his glasses and rubs at his brow for a moment. He looks tired. I wonder how many patients with CF he sees a day and whether they're all wise-cracking and sarcastic like me, or whether he has kids weeping and sobbing all over his desk. I note that he's got a box of white tissues with the top one sticking out in my direction like he's predicted I'm going to need it.

Tissues always remind me of the soft layer you find stuck underneath an almond macaroon. I love macaroons, the way when you bite into them they're chewy instead of crisp. I love the way that the sugar slightly grates the roof of your mouth while it dissolves and then there's the strange delight of eating edible paper from the bottom of the biscuit.

'No, not really,' he says. 'Of course you must carry on with the physio – that's very important. But the further deterioration of your lungs is hard for us to prevent. You may find it hard to walk anywhere much soon without oxygen and I guess that's going to have quite an impact on your quality of life, as well as on your schoolwork.'

I picture the school football team and a lump comes into my throat. Then I picture myself travelling up to London on the train for the competition, only the girl I'm picturing in the train carriage is bursting with vibrant health and doesn't have CF at all. She's a little on the plump side, but toned and athletic too. Her hair is thick and glossy with health rather than dry from lack of nutrients. She's a bit taller than I am – well, a lot taller. She's nearly as tall as a supermodel. Her skin is back to a normal light olive colour rather than pasty white and when she takes a deep breath she smiles and relaxes rather than burst into fits of rattling cough. The only thing she has to worry about is baking her best and looking good on TV.

Oh bother. Now I'm getting tears coming up into my eyes. I can't even look at Mum. I know exactly what her face will look like. She'll be biting her lip to try and stay in control and sensible and adult. Her eyes will be kind of imploring Mr Rogers to say something helpful and positive and not-too-scary.

We both know what he's going to say next. He said it last year at my annual review too, only then he said that we probably had another year or two before we needed to seriously consider it.

'I think we should speak again about putting you on the transplant list,' he says.

And with that the entire bottom falls out of my world, except that the way I see it in my head is somebody getting a huge sack of flour and then stabbing it at the bottom with a big knife so that all the flour trickles out and blows away.

'Mel, what do you think?' says Mum, reaching out to hold my hand.

They wait for me to answer.

I just can't speak.

On the way home I eat a Mars Bar in the passenger seat while Mum negotiates the rush-hour traffic. The CF centre is only ten miles from where we live, as Mum had all this in mind when she chose the house we live in now, but with the traffic it takes an hour to get back.

Neither of us says much in the car.

There's not really that much to say.

After Mr Rogers mentioned the transplant we spent another session in his office talking it all through and we decided that I would have to put my name on the list.

I don't have much choice really.

If I want to live for a good while longer, I've got to have it done. Time is running out.

Mum indicates and pulls in through the old stable arch and into our parking space at the back.

We sit in the car in silence for a moment, trying to find the right words.

In the end I try to make light of it because Mum looks so stricken.

'S'pose London's off, then?' I say. My voice sounds like a baby lamb, all thin and bleating. The thought of lamb makes a thin rush of hunger rise up in my chest, despite everything. Perhaps I'll see if there's any lamb mince in the freezer and make burgers instead of fish and chips. Burgers with blue cheese melted on top and thick, chunky fries and home-made tomato sauce. Yum.

Mum turns to face me. She takes both my hands in her thin, cold ones.

'Yes, Amelie,' she says. 'I'm really sorry, but you're just not up to it at the moment. London is most definitely off. End of story.'

She gets out of the car.

I follow her inside in silence.

Chapter Nine

After the annual review I spend a week feeling miserable.

My health continues to get worse. I struggle for breath and it's an effort to get to school. The school nurse keeps an eye on me, but she hasn't got time to single out one pupil for special attention, so mostly I monitor my own health and take pills and puffs of inhaler whenever I think I need them. I get the bus home and walk slowly up the road from the bus stop feeling like an OAP, all tired and out of breath. Sometimes Gemma walks with me. I've told her about the annual review and I could see the sympathy in her eyes mixed with relief that it wasn't all happening to her. I suppose most people that know me feel like that so I can't really blame her.

I've started to have some thoughts about Gemma and I don't like the way in which they are going. I've admitted to myself that I'm the tiniest bit jealous of her being so well all the time. She never even seems to catch a cold. And she's my best friend, so when I get these feelings I feel all swamped with guilt and self-loathing.

A date comes through for the day surgery to fit my gastrostomy so that I can have night feeds through a tube. It's for next week – one day before I was due to go to London.

Don't suppose it really matters now. I've got to have the tube, and that's that.

And as for the lung transplant, I just have to wait.

I could be waiting for years. A lot of people are on the waiting list and I need both lungs replacing rather than just one. I try not to think about what getting a new pair of lungs means but it's hard not to.

It means that somebody else will have to die so that I can breathe again.

That's one heck of a thought to carry around. I start to worry that if I have a different pair of lungs, I won't be me any longer. What if I take on the personality of the girl or boy who has died? What if they hated baking? What if I lose my Flour Power?

The thought is too terrifying to spend much time on.

And there's another thing which is making me sad.

I haven't heard from Harry.

I hang around the house all weekend annoying Mum by making mess in the kitchen and coming out with dramatic statements about lung transplants, until in the end she goes out shopping with a friend and leaves me alone for a couple of hours with strict instructions to ring her mobile if I feel worse. The door shuts behind her and it feels good for a moment to finally have her out of my hair but then the silence starts cutting in and I wander about the house coughing and looking out of windows and wondering if I'll ever hear from Harry again.

There's nothing on TV so I reach for my laptop and go on Facebook for a bit and then I don't know what makes me do this, because I know full well that the whole London thing is off and that Mum is expecting me to write to the competition organisers and tell them, but I go onto my blog and I see with a little thrill that there are twenty-six new replies to my post calling for recipe ideas. I click onto the first one. It's from somebody called Jules. This is what it says:

Just saw your blog entry and wanted to wish you loads of luck if you do get to the London competition. I'm one of the other people who applied but I didn't get through, so I wondered if you would like one of my recipes? You said you were looking for a biscuit recipe, right? Well, I'm letting you have my brilliant recipe for chewy macaroons. It's handed down from my grandmother. She's kind of mad, but I know she would be pleased if you cooked her recipe in the competition. Hope you win! Jules.

Macaroons! They only happen to be my most favourite biscuit in the entire world!

I scroll down the page and look at the recipe, my eyes glinting and my heart pounding. I print it off and then read the rest of the replies on my blog. Most of them are from teenage girls, but one or two are from boys. That's really cool, that boys have taken the trouble to get recipes from their families for me. There are masses of recipes for sticky, gooey cakes, including gingerbread and double chocolate brownies – yum. And somebody has even taken up my challenge to make a chocolate fondant and has posted a fuzzy photograph of chocolate sauce oozing out of soft sponge. Lots of people have expressed their disappointment that I might not be able to go to the competition. Yeah. Tell me about it. So I post a reply to every person who's given me a recipe and I print the recipes all out and am about to go downstairs and lie on the sofa with them and a big red pen and then a new blog response right at the top of the page catches my eye.

Dear Mel, You sound nice so I thought I'd give you one of my recipes. This is how you make it. You take one amazing, special girl with CF and you introduce her to a stupid idiot boy who forgets about all the good times that he has had with the amazing girl. Throw in his complete obsession with her awesome cupcakes and mix up together. The end result should be that the girl and the boy live together in perfect harmony, only the boy's got the recipe a bit wrong and has caused it to burn. Or curdle. Or whatever cake mix does – I mean, how would I know? I'm into sports, right? Anyway, hope you can use the recipe. Oh – and – SORRY. Hx

My eyes well up with tears. I look at the date – yesterday.

Then I pick up my mobile phone and wait for his lovely kind voice to answer.

Something happens to me that evening.

After I speak to Harry and he says he's missed me and he's sorry (again), I feel all fired up and strange and a little bit reckless.

Mum has come back home laden with shopping bags and we get out all the clothes she's bought and try them on. She's got me some new black leggings and a pretty summer tunic top in white with red roses on it.

'It's brilliant, Mum,' I say, twirling in front of the mirror and then stopping to cough. 'Thanks. And I'm sorry I've been a nightmare daughter this week.'

'Only this week?' says Mum, but her eyes are glinting in a naughty sort of way. She's bought cream cakes home too and we devour them at the kitchen table with a cup of proper coffee and for once we don't talk about how my own recipes would be better or about CF or the competition or school, but just enjoy cramming the pastry into our mouths and licking the cream off our lips.

'It's good having a daughter who doesn't tell me off about extra calories,' says Mum, reaching for another cake and undoing her brown leather belt. 'I might even order a Chinese later too. What do you think?'

'Great,' I say, but I'm not really listening.

I don't know whether it's the cake, or the kindness of all the strangers with their recipes, or the fact I've been resting at home for days, or that Harry was so sweet on the phone and I'm relieved that we're going out again, or maybe even that deep down I realise I might be on course to a lung transplant and am going to be out of action for ages – but my brain is doing all these strange, devious little things that I can't voice to Mum. The more I try and ignore them, the bigger and more powerful they seem to get, until I feel like I'm going to burst if I don't go upstairs to my bedroom and give them some serious thought.

'I'm tired,' I lie as we clear up. 'Might go to bed for a bit. I'll get up for supper, don't worry.'

'Oh,' says Mum. Her jolly voice has faded back to the concerned one again. 'Are you sure you're OK? You never go to bed in the day.'

'Yeah,' I say. 'I'm just going to lie on the bed and watch TV in my room, that's all.'

'Ah, right,' says Mum. Her smile returns. 'One of your dreadful teen soaps, no doubt.'

'Of course,' I say. 'Or a cookery programme. That's new, right?'

Mum laughs and takes her bags upstairs. I follow her and go into my room.

I shut the door and wait until she's gone downstairs again and I hear her chatting on the phone to my grandmother.

Then I lift the lid of the laptop and start to hatch my plan.

Chapter Ten

For the next five days I go about my usual business, but
I've got this bubbling excitement inside me and it's all I
can do not to blurt it out to anybody.

It's like the secret I'm carrying around has given me a
new burst of energy. I stay at school full-time all week and
I take part in another football match and only need my
inhaler once after the game and not before like I usually
do. I go to the cinema with Harry after school on the
Monday and I sit all snuggled up under his arm in the
back row and I feel like I might die from happiness and
excitement rather than from CF, which is a new way of
looking at things.

I update my blog when I get home from seeing Harry,
before I do my tedious physio session on the bed.

I chew my pen and think carefully about the words I

am going to use. I mean – what if Mum saw my blog? Not that she ever would. But just in case. So I just write this:

Hi, it's Amelie here. I haven't really got an update about the competition because like I said before, Mum has made it clear that I can't go to London because it would be bad for my health.

And because I know she's right, I probably ought to listen to her... probably...

I leave it at that. When I log on again an hour later, there's a reply from a girl called Jen. It says:

Whoo-hoo, girl! I'm sensing a cake rebellion. Keep us posted, won't you? Jen. P.S. My chocolate fondant sunk like a stone so I won't put a picture of it here.

Somewhere deep inside me a little voice is telling me that I'm storing up harm for myself by throwing myself around as if there was nothing wrong with me, but I choose to ignore it.

Mum is pleased to see me being so much more energetic, but when she thinks I'm not looking, I catch her giving me puzzled glances and then almost speaking but thinking better of it.

At the end of the week she's obviously decided she can't keep it to herself any longer.

We're sitting in front of the television devouring a plate of my strawberry and banana muffins and watching a comedy that we both like. When the adverts come on,

Mum leans forward and clicks the mute button on the remote.

'Amelie,' she says, turning to me with a frown. She's wearing a fluffy pink dressing gown and slippers and her hair is up in a towel. Mum always has Bath Night on a Friday when she gets home from work. I'm still wearing my school uniform, but I've removed the horrid tie and black patent shoes and let my blouse hang out over my skirt.

'What?' I say. I haven't really been concentrating on the telly. My head is a blur of ideas, plans and a fair number of devious lies that I am going to have to tell pretty soon.

'Well,' says Mum. 'I just wondered if there's anything going on that you're not telling me about? Because since the annual review you've been kind of jumpy and restless and although you're eating and sleeping and looking better, I'm wondering if some of it's a bit of an act?'

Our programme comes back on and I make a move towards the remote, but Mum grabs it from me and puts it under her bottom.

'Health is more important,' she says. 'So? I'm waiting.'

A whole load of conflicting thoughts are crashing about in my head. Part of me badly wants to tell Mum. Even though she drives me mad at times, she's still the person who is most on my side in the whole world, more even than Harry. He doesn't see me at my worse, when I'm being sick and hooked up to machines and yelling at Mum out of misery and frustration. Mum has seen it all for years and years and she is still here caring for me.

But if I tell her she will morph into The CF Police again and my plan will be trampled into the mud.

I play for time by reaching out for another muffin and dissecting it into soft lumps on my plate. I've used giant, moist strawberries and bananas just at the peak of their ripeness, along with a load of butter and sugar from Karim's shop. I managed to do two hours after school last night and didn't need to sit down and catch my breath for once.

'Amelie,' she says. 'Will you just tell me what's going on, for God's sake? I wouldn't mind going to bed this side of midnight.'

Uh-oh. Mum getting sarcastic is never a good sign. It's usually followed by a flare-up of anger and the slamming of doors.

I stretch and give her my best smile.

'Nothing is going on,' I say. 'I'm just happy. I'm back with Harry and I feel a bit better. I'm allowed to be happy, aren't I?'

Mum's face softens. She reaches out and touches my hair.

'Of course, love,' she says. 'I just want you to know that you can always talk to me. About, you know, the way that CF makes you feel. OK?'

'OK,' I say, eating the last bit of muffin and slurping down my hot chocolate. Mum's put a swirl of cream and some chocolate flakes on top just to get in as many calories as possible.

'Night,' says Mum, getting up. 'Oh – you've had your

Creon? And done your breathing?'

I give a deep, impatient sigh.

'Yeah, yeah,' I say. 'I don't want Tom to give me another lecture.'

Mum smiles and clicks off the kitchen light.

'Oh – and Amelie,' she says as she starts going upstairs. 'Don't forget that we're going to hospital on Monday for you to have your gastrostomy fitted. I've told the school you'll be off for a couple of days.'

'Righty ho,' I say. Then I wonder why I've said that. I sound about ninety. It's hard to get Mum off my case sometimes.

I go upstairs to my room and shut the door.

Then I perch in the middle of the bed and log onto my laptop. I put in my passwords and check my online savings account.

'Wow,' I say. There's five hundred pounds in there, from various birthday and Christmas presents. I hardly ever buy clothes or make-up, like most of the girls in my class, and I get my ingredients from Karim so I don't often need to buy too many of them either.

'Good,' I say to myself. 'That should cover everything.'

I get under the duvet, but it's hot and I'm too fired up to sleep so after a while I get up again and find a book but I can't even concentrate on that.

In the end I just lie on top of the duvet staring up at the white ceiling and practising recipes in my head until I must have fallen asleep, because I wake up in the same position six hours later and it's Saturday.

Mornings are not good when you've got CF. All the gunk in your chest seems to get harder and thicker overnight and you wake up with a heavy, clogged feeling that's difficult to shift.

I stay on the bed and do my breathing cycle for forty minutes until I've pushed loads of mucus up out of my airways. When I first started doing the physio myself, forty minutes felt like a lifetime to be trapped on a bed without getting up, but now I hardly notice. Then I rest for five minutes, swing my legs over the side of the bed and get dressed in my leggings, a white tunic top and silver ballet shoes. I brush my long black hair and let it fall over my shoulders. I study my face in the mirror. I'm always pale because of my CF, but today there's a tiny flush of colour in my cheeks.

I'm meeting Gemma in town and I'm going to let her in on my secret.

It's a big one.

And I need her help.

'You're crazy,' says Gemma.

We're sitting in McDonalds and stuffing burgers and chips. I've got two burgers both with cheese on and a double portion of fries and a strawberry milkshake. Gemma's got some weird chicken burger with salad in it and a small portion of fries.

I click the plastic lid off my milkshake and stir the thick gloop around with my red straw.

'I'm not crazy,' I say. 'I'm just ambitious. I need to do

this. It's part of the rest of my life, what's left of it.'

Gemma screws up her face and nibbles on the end of a chip.

'Your mum is going to kill you anyway when she finds out,' she says. 'So I reckon you won't need to worry about CF shortening your life any longer.'

'Ha ha,' I say, but my determined smile is fading. I've been trying not to picture Mum's face when she finds out. I can't afford to think about it. If I do, I'll be swamped with horrid guilt and have to call the whole thing off. Besides, it's too late now. I've gone so far with the planning that I couldn't go back now even if I wanted to.

'What did you want me to do?' says Gemma. 'Because I'm not so sure I should be backing you up on this. What about if you get really sick and there's nobody to help you? Maybe I should come with.'

I pull a piece of slimy lettuce out of my burger and sigh. If I was making this same meal at home I'd have done the burger out of lean beef and shaped into thick, juicy rounds. I'd have served it in a home-made bun with masses of organic roast tomatoes and with loads of good French mustard.

'Never mind the burger,' says Gemma, reading my mind. She knows me so well. 'Do you want me to come with you?'

I put down my burger and switch to the fries instead. They're OK, I suppose, but they don't really taste of potato, just of fat and salt. Still, it's all calories. I shovel them in and give Gemma my best smile.

'That's really nice of you,' I say. 'But then my mother will kill you as well, or probably your own mother will kill you. So there would be two tragic deaths. Maybe we ought to keep it to just one, yeah?'

I expect Gemma to laugh, but she looks mournful and pushes the remains of her meal in my direction.

'I wish you didn't have CF,' she says. 'It sucks.'

'You're telling me,' I say, biting into her chicken burger and pulling a face at the dry, stringy chicken inside the bun. 'But there's not much I can do about that. Except I really, really want to do this. And I need you to pretend that I'm coming round yours on Sunday night to do homework. OK?'

Gemma nods.

'OK,' she says. 'But when your mum realises, she's going to call me, isn't she? What do I say then?'

'I'm leaving her a note,' I say. 'Just tell her to read it. And tell her it was me who put you up to it. She won't be cross with you then. I just need to get to London before she knows, that's all.'

Gemma sighs and finishes off her fries.

'Are you going to tell Harry?' she says. 'Maybe he could go with you.'

I've already thought about that.

'I don't think I can tell him,' I say. 'I think he'd side with Mum. Say I wasn't up to it.'

Gemma nods. She knows how protective Harry can be. The three of us have a lot of fun when we hang out, but she sees Harry watching my face for signs of tiredness and checking that I've had my pills, even though he doesn't do it in such an obvious way as Mum.

'You're a bit of a nightmare, Amelie Day,' she says. 'You and your Flour Power.'

I grin at her.

'I need to buy another new dress,' I say. 'Come on. You're good at that.'

We leave arm in arm and head deeper into the precinct.

I spend two hours trying on different dresses in different shops and Gemma and I can't agree on which ones look good and which ones don't. But in the end we both agree on a white flippy sundress with a brown cut-off cardigan over the top and a pair of brown ballerina pumps with little leather flowers on them.

'It looks good but also you won't fall over in it,' says Gemma as I get out the wad of cash that I took out of the machine earlier and pay for the things. 'And you'll probably have an apron over the whole lot anyway, won't you?'

'I guess so,' I say. I sit down and cough. My newfound energy is starting to flag a bit now and I've got a small thrill of fear in my stomach. Now I've bought the outfit it feels like this is really going to happen. And I don't know what to expect at all, other than that I've got to be there on Monday at 9 in the morning.

And that I'm travelling up to London on my own.

Chapter Eleven

On Sunday afternoon Dad comes over to see me.

'I really hope it goes well tomorrow, Mel,' he says. We're sitting outside in our courtyard garden on the cobbles where horses used to tread. Sometimes it's weird thinking that I live inside a building where horses were tied up and taken out to hook up to old carriages. Once or twice at night I swear I've heard the neigh of a horse and the stamping of hoofs, but I reckon I'm probably just imagining it.

'What?' I say with a start. I'm half asleep today. Couldn't sleep at all last night for mulling it all over in my head. For a moment I think that he's rumbled me. Then I realise that he's referring to my operation. I wish I could tell Dad where I'm really going. I know that he's keen for me to follow my heart and my cooking and try to fulfil all my ambitions while I've still got enough breath to do them. I also know that he'd be very angry if I did something behind Mum's back.

That's why I can't risk telling him.

'Oh, thanks,' I say in what I hope is a vague way. I need to change the subject. Quick.

'I've made treacle tarts,' I say. 'Little ones. Do you want some?'

Dad stretches out in the sun on his chair and makes a noise of satisfaction.

'Now you're talking,' he says. 'What are you waiting for? Bring on the cake!'

I go inside to get a tea tray together. Mum is in the kitchen watering all her houseplants. The sight of her back and the way that she's humming as she waters makes guilty tears threaten to spring up in my throat. For a moment I feel really small. Then I have a feeling of genuine fear. This is my home, the place where I feel safe and Mum looks after me. And I'm going to remove myself from my safety zone and throw myself into the Great Unknown, all on my own.

'They look nice,' says Mum, turning round and watching me put the mini-tarts onto a big white plate. I've put strips of criss-cross pastry across the glistening orange tops of each little tart. I can already feel the way that the treacle is going to glue all our teeth together. 'Save me one. I'll be out in a minute. Oh – maybe we can take the rest to hospital tomorrow, for after the op? You know how you hate hospital food.'

'Mm,' I say, ducking back out through the back door into the courtyard.

Dad bites into my crumbly pastry and gooey treacle with an exclamation of bliss.

'You really are good at this, aren't you?' he says, letting crumbs fall all over his blue shirt. 'It's a shame you can't get to that competition. I reckon you'd have done really well.'

He rolls up his shirt-sleeves and lies back in the sun with his eyes closed. I dissect the strips of pastry from the top of my tart and suck on them, but I'm not really thinking about the recipe for once. All I can think of is what I've got to do later.

I hope that it works.

I do my breathing at six after Dad's gone and then I make sure that my tablet box has everything I'm going to need in it. I drag out my rucksack from under my bed and I pack the box, the inhaler, the nebuliser and a plastic bowl in case I need to throw up. The oxygen canister is too big and bulky for me to manage so I leave it at home.

I feel sick already but I reckon that's just nerves.

I add the new dress, cardigan and shoes to my bag, along with the grey tunic that Mum bought me and pack a pair of leggings, a pair of jeans and a couple of vests and t-shirts. Then I put in a bottle of water and several packets of crisps and bars of chocolate. At the top I put a couple of my treacle tarts in a plastic box and at the very top I put my pink leather purse stuffed to the brim with money.

Then I do the zip up with some effort and stuff the bag under my bed.

I'm just in time. Mum comes in without knocking.

'Is Gemma's mum feeding you?' she says. 'Or will you be back for supper?'

'Feeding me,' I say. It's frightening how good I'm getting at this lying business.

Mum smiles. 'It's beans on toast and Coronation Street for me then,' she says. 'Hooray.'

I wait until I hear her go into the bathroom and then I sneak downstairs with my rucksack and go out to the front garden. I hide the rucksack behind the green recycling bin and come back inside again.

Mum comes downstairs with a pile of washing in her arms.

'Are you off, love?' she says. 'Don't be late back. Remember we're up early for hospital tomorrow.'

'Yeah, I just need to get my stuff,' I say, bolting upstairs again. I go into Mum's room and creep over to the bed. I get a letter out of my bag and put it on her pillow. Then I cover the pillow a bit with her duvet and creep out again.

I pick up a small black leather bag from my room and grab a couple of school exercise books so that Mum can see them.

Then I go downstairs to say goodbye.

Mum gives me a big kiss.

'You're being very brave about tomorrow,' she says. 'You must be a bit nervous. I know I am.'

My heart gives a big pang. I don't much like lying to Mum. Then again I wouldn't know how to stop this now. It's gone too far.

I take a quick look at the cosy lounge, at the cream sofa where I lie when I'm not feeling well, at the TV I spend so many hours staring at and then over Mum's shoulder to the kitchen where all my pans and trays and ingredients live.

A pang of something horrid comes up into my throat and for once it's not mucus.

I force a smile onto my face.

'See you later, Mum,' I say.

Then I go outside, hide my exercise books behind the bin, grab my rucksack from the front garden and head off down the road.

Chapter Twelve

I walk to the station.

It takes about twenty minutes and all the time I'm looking around to see if any of Mum's friends or neighbours are about to drive past and rumble me, but they don't.

It's a steep walk up the hill as the road nears the station and I feel the familiar tightness in my chest so I sit down on a bench for a moment and catch my breath, take a deep puff on my inhaler. Then I hoist the rucksack onto my back, cross the busy main road and go into the station.

The station is quite small and there aren't many people around on Sunday evening. I approach the ticket desk feeling as if I'm on a secret spy mission or something.

'Ticket to London, please,' I say, dropping the rucksack onto the ground. I forgot how heavy it was going to be with all my medicine in. At the last moment I put in some little bottles of high-calorie milk drinks but they're really weighing me down.

'Single or return?' says the guy behind the counter.

I consider this for a moment.

'Don't know yet,' I say. It all depends whether I bomb out at the first stage of the quarter-finals on Monday or whether I go through to the semi-finals which are being filmed on Wednesday. 'Single, I s'pose.'

'That'll be forty-four pounds then,' says the guy. A couple of little orange tickets whiz out of a machine and are slid under the glass towards me.

I nearly pass out when he says this. Forty-four pounds!

'Is there a cheaper ticket?' I say. 'That's kind of a lot.'

The man laughs.

'When did you last go to London?' he says. 'That's a standard off-peak rate. It costs more than that during the week.'

I flush. I haven't been on the train to London for at least a year and last time Mum came with and bought the tickets.

I shove my money-box cash in his direction and put the tickets in the front of my purse. Then I hoist up the rucksack again and go to wait on the platform.

I've got five minutes. I take out a bottle of high-cal milk and drink it while I'm waiting. Then I start on a bag of crisps.

The train pulls in and I heave my bag onto it and find a seat. As soon as I sit down a great wave of tiredness and relief comes over me. I've done it. I'm actually on the train to London.

The carriage is pretty empty so I get all my food out and arrange it around me. I take my Creon and then eat a sandwich that I made up this morning while Mum wasn't looking. I finish up with a Mars Bar and then put the food away in the rucksack. Then I put all my medical stuff into my small black leather bag so that I've got it all together and I put it on the seat next to me. I prop up my feet on the rucksack and get out my list of recipe notes so that I can start rehearsing how to bake them in my head.

The train lurches and sways through countryside. It's very hot and I feel exhausted. I lean my head against the window for a moment and watch all the trees and fields whiz by in a blur. Don't suppose it matters if I have a bit of a rest. I'm going to need all my energy for what lies ahead.

The next thing I know I'm jolting awake with my head banging on the glass and a horrid dry feeling in my mouth.

It takes me a while to remember where I am. My head is aching and my chest feels tight. It's like the past few days of plotting and planning kept me going. Now that the excitement of being secretive has gone, I feel like I've been in a fight. And lost.

I yawn and look at my watch. I must have been asleep for nearly an hour because there's only twenty minutes left until the train gets in. I get out a little mirror from the top pocket of my rucksack and then attempt to calm down my hair. My face looks thin and pale in the early evening sunlight, but I try to ignore that. I get a bottle of water out and another snack and then turn to get my black leather bag full of medicine so that I can take some more Creon.

It's gone.

I'm bolt awake now.

I search under the seat, behind the seat and on all the other empty seats around me. Then I open my rucksack just in case I'm going mad and put the little bag back in there without thinking, but it's not there either.

My heart pounds with fright and uncertainty. I don't know what to do now.

I check in my rucksack for my phone and money and they're still there, at least. Thank God I didn't put them in the little bag. But who can I call? Mum isn't supposed to know where I am yet and my train is almost in London. I don't know a single soul in London.

I try to think, even though tears are rising up and threatening to spill over.

Maybe I could find a chemist in London and tell them I've lost my drugs? But then they'd be bound to contact my GP's surgery and they in turn would have to contact Mum and then the game would be up.

I could call Gemma, but I couldn't expect her to come all the way up to London having first somehow got into my house and gone upstairs to my bedroom and got all my spare medicine and come out again. And anyway I don't want to switch my phone on in case Mum or Harry call and then my voice will sound guilty and give the game away.

I'm shivering, even though the train is stuffy and the air-con isn't working. This so wasn't supposed to happen. I'm angry with myself for leaving the little bag on the seat next to me and then falling asleep. Somebody must have thought it contained money. That's why they took it.

I sit there swearing and cursing and thinking, but I can't come up with any good solution.

No.

I'm going to have to try and get through the next three days without my meds.

I've never had to do that before. If I eat meals without Creon I get the worst stomach aches ever. If I get out of breath and have no inhaler I might possibly faint or choke.

Or die.

I feel really scared now.

I cling onto my rucksack.

The train grinds into Waterloo and comes to a screeching halt.

Chapter Thirteen

I'd forgotten how busy London can be.

Once I've dragged my rucksack off the train and got it back onto my aching shoulders I stand on the platform disorientated and dizzy as people rush past me and bang into my back and sides. They're like a swarm of ants all trying to run in different directions.

Dazed, I walk towards the ticket barrier. My rucksack gets caught in the automatic gates and I have to go backwards and try again and then my ticket is spat out of the slot and a beeping noise comes out of the machine. A man behind me tuts and gestures in the direction of the ticket inspector.

'He'll let you through.'

I push my way through to the gates on the end. Everybody else seems to be shoving and barging in, so I decide I might as well join in. I get a lot of rude noises and glares from the people I'm hitting with my rucksack, but I'm beyond caring.

All I want to do is get to the hotel and draw the curtains, lie on the bed and cry.

First I've got to negotiate the tube.

I put my rucksack down in front of me on the escalator, but it sticks out and nearly trips up the people rushing down the inside. I lift it up and try to hold it in front of me but my chest is hurting and I'm struggling to breathe. At the foot of the escalator I have to stop to put it on my back again and a load of people behind nearly catapult over my head.

'Great place to stop, you stupid girl,' says a woman in high heels. She clicks off, swinging her briefcase and shaking her head in annoyance.

I fight back tears. I'd give anything to see a friendly face – Mum, Harry, even any kid from school – but that's not really likely down here in the smelly bowels of the London Underground, so I drag myself off to find the Northern Line after a quick look at the directions I printed off earlier.

The tube is packed to the brim with people, even though it's Sunday evening. Most of them look like tourists. They're holding rucksacks like mine or staring at the map of the underground above my head and shouting at one another in loud, foreign voices.

I stand with my hand on the greasy pole in the middle of the carriage and try not to panic. Mum's always told me to keep away from the underground because it's a hotbed of germs and viruses and with CF I spend most of my time trying not to catch anything. We used to live in London but Mum moved out when she and Dad broke up and her main reason was because of the increased risk of infection.

I push my way off and change onto the Piccadilly Line. My B&B is in a part of London called Bloomsbury. I chose it on the internet because it looked close to the studio where the baking competition is going to be filmed. I reckoned that 'Bloomsbury' sounded cool – kind of pretty and old-fashioned with lots of cherry trees and cobbled squares.

Yeah, right.

There's a horrid lift at Russell Square station and I have to cram into it with loads of other bleary-eyed people all trying not to look at one another. The lift judders, stops, starts and creaks to ground level, before we're all spewed out into the station and then out into the humid, stale-smelling London air.

I slide my rucksack off my shoulders to give them a rest. Then I look left and right and consult the map I printed off the Net this morning. The roads are crammed with traffic and people and I can't see the street names at first, so I set off in what I hope is the right direction and after about five minutes of struggle I end up at a small grey concrete building that sits at one end of a square with railings around it. There's a flight of steps leading up to the front door and I just can't face them at the moment so I cross the road and go to find a bench in the square.

There's a statue of a woman's head in one corner. She's got a beaky nose and a thin, sad-looking face. The head is made of bronze and is covered in pigeon droppings. I look at the plaque underneath. It's somebody called 'Virginia Woolf' and she used to live in a building on this square. She looks about as miserable as I feel. I wonder if she had CF?

I sit next to Virginia, lean back and drink loads of water from one of my bottles. I feel like I need a snack but I'm scared to eat too much without my Creon, so I nibble on the corner of a Mars Bar and then fold the wrapper back over the rest and put it away again.

I drag myself back over the road and up the stairs into the B&B reception.

The building is very modern. When I booked it I pictured an old-fashioned Victorian sort of building, with hanging baskets and a friendly woman on reception with maybe a hotel cat perched on the desk.

There's nobody at the small reception desk inside the door, so I ping the bell and wait.

A dark-haired woman with olive skin and large gold earrings shuffles down the hallway in a pair of oversized fluffy slippers.

'Yes, love?' she says.

'I'm booked in for three nights,' I say, breathless. 'I think.'

I don't really know. It all depends whether I get past the quarter-finals tomorrow.

'You look very young,' says the woman.

'I'm nearly sixteen,' I say, drawing myself up as tall as my short body will allow me to. I put my purse on the desk and raise my eyebrows at her, tapping my fingertips on the polished wood in what I hope is a grown-up, impatient fashion.

'I'm booked in,' I say again. 'Melanie Smith.' It's all part of my mega-plan of deception. I don't want anybody ringing up this B&B and somehow finding out that I'm here. Or at least – I didn't. None of this seems quite such a good idea now that I've lost all my medication.

My chest is making the noises that mean that any moment now I'm going to start to cough and not be able to stop.

The woman gives me a small smile. I reckon I look pretty pale and washed up.

'You're checked in,' she says. 'You pay when you check out. Breakfast is from eight until ten. Continental only, I'm afraid.'

The way my stomach's feeling, that's probably a good thing.

Then the woman hands me a key and tells me that my room is on the first floor.

There's no lift so I drag myself up the stairs, my lungs tugging on every step. I open the door to Room Eight and shut it behind me.

I stand by the bed and look around.

The room is very small. The double bed with its dull brown bedspread pretty much fills most of it. There's a tiny television on a table in one corner and a dressing table on the wall nearest the door. A white door leads into the smallest bathroom I've ever seen. There's no room for a bath, just a shower which drips onto a mat in the corner. On the shelf over the toilet are three tiny plastic bottles of shampoo and conditioner and a shower cap.

I stare around me at this dismal picture for a moment or two and try not to picture my pretty bedroom at home with its white soft duvet, oak desk and bedside lamp. Then I open the zip on my rucksack.

'Might as well unpack,' I say, although there's nobody to say it to. I hang up my new dress in the cramped wardrobe and put my t-shirts and jeans on a shelf inside it. Then I arrange all my snacks and drinks on the little table by the bed.

'Too bad I won't be able to eat you,' I say to them. My stomach is growling with hunger and anxiety all at once.

I get my recipe notebook out and perch cross-legged on the bed, with my hair half-falling over my face. I run through what I've got to do a couple of times until I feel more confident. I had to email the television studio about two weeks ago with a list of all the ingredients I'm going to use and I'm hoping that they've got everything I need.

At ten o'clock I stop and lie down. My chest feels tight and clogged and I'm missing my inhaler already. I look at my mobile but can't bring myself to switch it on. Round about now Mum will call Gemma to ask why I'm not back yet, because we've got hospital in the morning. And Gemma will have to confess her part in all this and tell Mum to go and read the note on her pillow.

I feel sick with a sense of my own daring when I think of Mum reading that note.

'Breathing,' I say to myself. 'At least I can still do that.'

I lie on my back and do forty minutes of the autogenic drainage exercises like Tom showed me. The rattling in my chest is dreadful today. I don't think that CF reacts very well to stress.

After I've finished my exercises I eat a couple of biscuits and eye up the treacle tarts that I made yesterday. They look good cold, but I know if I eat too much without Creon I'm going to be in agony in the middle of the night. I eat one bite from one of the tarts and then wrap it up again. I drink another high-calorie milk drink from one of my little bottles and then I get into my sleep t-shirt and huddle under the thin bedcovers, with the cheap curtains doing a bad job of blocking out any light.

Down below my room London continues to roar with life right into the next morning. The traffic in the square hoots and roars and brakes squeal. About a million fire engines blaze past with their sirens blaring every half an hour or so, right through the night.

At three in the morning I get up again and have another drink. My stomach feels tender when I press it and I'm struggling a bit for breath. I sit by the window and gaze down on the lights of London until I feel tired.

Then I hop back into bed and at last fall asleep just before it's time to get up.

When I wake in the morning I do my breathing again and put on the small plastic kettle that I found inside my wardrobe. I make myself a cup of coffee with sugar in it to try and make up for the lack of sleep.

I get out my best red t-shirt and skinny jeans and lay them on the bed while I take a shower. The water only seems to come out lukewarm, but I haven't really got any other option, so I wash as best as I can and use the free conditioner on my hair because I've left my own bottle at home.

All the time I'm getting ready I hum loudly. I'm trying to block out the thoughts of Mum that keep popping into my head. She'll be furious. And worried out of her mind, and embarrassed because she'll have to call the hospital and tell them that I won't be coming in for my operation after all.

At least she won't be able to find my B&B. I didn't even tell Gemma where I was staying. And I hid the letter with the details of the competition on them in a hope that Mum won't have remembered where it was taking place.

I make a face at myself in the mirror. I look dreadful. My skin is white and dry and there are dark furrows under each eye. My hair has gone lank from the cheap conditioner and I swear my face looks thinner than it did yesterday. I wish I could eat.

I wish I hadn't lost my black leather bag on the train.

I manage a few squares of dark chocolate with my coffee. That will have to do for breakfast. I've got to get to the studios by half-past nine and it's already nearly nine.

I stuff my purse, phone and recipe lists into one of my pockets and two bottles of milk drink into the other. I haven't got a small bag to carry my stuff in and I don't really want to turn up to the competition with that enormous rucksack on my back so it will have to do.

I take a last look round the poky room and leave it with relief. I get the lift downstairs, go past reception and out into the bewildering mess and noise of Bloomsbury. I search about a bit and find a line of black taxis so I get into one trying to look as if I know what I'm doing and I give the driver the address of the studios. Then I sit back and attempt to look like a healthy, confident and streetwise London girl who hops into black cabs every single day. I see the driver look at me once or twice in the mirror and I know that this is not what he's seeing, but I keep a silly fixed smile on my face and look about the streets with what I hope is a knowing sort of look on my face.

The cab ride costs over twenty quid which seems a lot for such a short ride, but I pay it with the same smile on my face and then turn round and prance into the building in front of me as if I've known it all my life.

I find myself standing in a vast glass entrance hall with a shiny black desk right at the very end of it. There's a blonde woman sitting behind it so I go and give her my name and she writes me out a plastic badge and tells me to put it on and wait on the black sofas.

I sink into the soft black leather and gaze up at the giant TV screens in front of me. Loads of trendy looking people rush into the reception area and flash their security passes at a machine to get into the main building behind it.

I sit with my legs clenched together, chewing my lip and looking around. Hope they haven't forgotten about me. I'm finding it hard to believe I actually made it to London all on my own, spent a night in a rubbish hotel and then found my way here.

'This is it,' I whisper to myself for confidence. 'Flour Power!'

I feel a bit better when I think of my favourite catchphrase, but not for long. There's the familiar, dreaded shifting in the centre of my chest and the feeling of something catching.

'Oh no,' I mutter. Then I double up with my head towards my knees and cough for England. The noise echoes around the vast polished entrance hall and seems to bounce off the white walls and come back to me, like a cough boomerang. People stare at me as they walk past but nobody stops.

I cough on and on. Can't seem to stop. I could do with my inhaler right now and a nice steadying breath of oxygen.

When I come up for air there's a woman standing over me with a look of concern on her face.

'Are you alright?' she says. 'You don't look terribly well.'

She's tall with blonde hair and has a name badge on which says 'Elaine McDonald, Floor Manager.' I glance at the shiny floors around us.

'Your floors look very well managed,' I say, trying to be polite, even though I'm finding it hard to catch my breath.

The woman stares at me for at a moment. Then she sees me looking at her name badge and bursts out laughing.

'Oh,' she says. 'I see. Well – actually I'm the floor manager in the studio. It means that I direct everybody as to what to do when the cameras are rolling. Make sure everyone is in the right place. Anyway, I take it you're here for *Best Teen Baker*? Don't you have a parent with you?'

I nod. My eyes are watering from the last bout of coughing but I stand up and shake the woman's hand.

'Nice to meet you,' I say. 'Sorry. I've just got over the flu. And my mum is coming along later.'

Wow. I could lie for the Olympic Games, I'm getting so good at it.

I follow Elaine into the black lifts at the back of the building and she takes me down endless long corridors and up more flights of stairs until I'm gasping for breath again but I do my best to hide it. We end up in a big space full of cooking stations and people setting up cameras and microphones.

'Here we are,' says Elaine. 'We'll be having a rehearsal when everybody's here. That means you'll get to run through your recipes before we start the cameras rolling. OK?'

I nod. That sounds like a good idea. I'm so tired and nervous that my brain has gone blank. I finger the recipe book in my pocket for comfort.

'The main competition will be filmed at four,' says Elaine. 'It won't go out on TV for a good few months yet. We get you to sign an agreement not to tell anybody about who gets through and who doesn't. That way the viewers keep watching TV to find out.'

I nod again. I like Elaine. She seems friendly and

capable. If only she also doubled up as a CF nurse and I could tell her I desperately need some oxygen. I catch a glimpse of my own reflection in the shiny door of the giant fridge on set and I swear that my lips are actually turning a bit blue round the edges.

'Can I get you a drink?' Elaine is saying. 'It's very hot outside. Great air con in here, though.'

In fact I feel frozen. Because I'm thinner than a girl my age should be, I feel cold even in the middle of summer. The air conditioning in here is sharp and vicious, blowing great gusty drafts of ice-cold air around my aching bones.

'Something warm would be good,' I say. Elaine sends another girl off with orders for a couple of coffees and then her attention is distracted by the arrival of another group of competitors, so I take the chance to sit on a stool and steady myself.

I take a look at the cooking stations. They're really cool. There are twelve of them dotted about the large studio, each with a built-in cooker and plenty of granite work surface for chopping and food preparation. Shiny steel spotlights are angled over each station and as I look around, a man comes in with a huge trolley and starts unloading ingredients. I recognise mine when he starts putting out a load of dark chocolate bars and sugar for my mini-chocolate fondant puddings, golden syrup and treacle for my sticky gingerbread and boxes of eggs and tubs of cream for my Chantilly crème and vanilla custard. Then he puts out flour, cocoa powder, chopped nuts, eggs and butter for my macaroons.

My heart gives a little thrill of excitement and nerves. I made it. I'm here. I'm actually going to take part in the competition!

That's if my chest doesn't seize up first.

It really hurts.

I'm trying to ignore the pain but I'm wondering if I've started another chest infection because my head feels a bit giddy and, although I'm shivering, my head is burning hot. I've lost my appetite, too. Even the thought of a biscuit makes me feel sick.

I gulp on the hot sugary cappuccino that Elaine's PA brings me and lick the froth off my lips. It's not as good as the ones I make at home but I feel a bit better, even though my stomach feels twisted and tender.

I wonder who it was who stole my leather bag?

I reckon they got one heck of a disappointment when they opened it and found a load of useless tablets and medical gadgets, rather than a big purse full of money or an expensive iPhone.

'Serves them right,' I mutter.

Then we're all beckoned over to the cooking stations with our ingredients on them.

I take a look at the other contestants.

There are five other girls and six boys, most of them about the same age as me although one or two look older. The girls look very assured and confident. They're all in jeans and pretty tops with shiny hair tied back into fluffy ponytails and loads of lipgloss.

I hadn't thought to put any make-up on for today.

My t-shirt is plain and red and boring. I was saving the best outfit for if I got through to the final. I tug at my hair and try to let it fall over my face in what I hope passes for a sophisticated and confident manner, but it just lies in lank strands over my shoulders.

I'm just wondering whether I should make the effort to go and talk to the other contestants, when Elaine bears down on me in a cloud of sickly perfume. Great. Another cough trigger.

'You'll have to tie that up,' she whispers, pointing at my hair and passing me an elastic band. 'Food hygiene, I'm afraid.'

I gather up my hair and shove it back into a thin pony-tail. I hate having my hair tied back so now I feel as if my pale, ill face is even more on show than it was before.

A whole load of new lights are flicked on. They're so bright that I almost can't see for a moment.

'OK, folks,' shouts a man behind a camera with a black and white board in his hand. 'We're doing a dummy run just to see how you all look on camera and to get you used to cooking on this equipment. Just relax and cook your best recipes. You've got two hours.'

Elaine is standing next to him with a clipboard in her hand. She gives us all the thumbs-up and the man shouts, 'AND... ACTION!' Before I know it I'm deep into measuring out flour and melting butter and treacle for my sticky German gingerbread.

I lose myself in what I'm doing. It's amazing, cooking in the TV studio with all the beautiful pots and shiny gadgets. I'm so immersed in the joy of it that I jump out of my skin when a buzzer sounds and the man behind the camera shouts, 'AND... CUT! Well done, everybody.'

Elaine comes over and has a word with each of us in turn.

When she reaches my station she smiles.

'You did very well, particularly if you've still got the flu,' she says. I know I'm looking pretty rough because I feel dreadful. 'So what will happen later at this stage is that the judges will call you forwards with your three dishes and they'll try a mouthful of each and tell you what they think. Then they'll decide who's going through to the semi. OK?'

She's about to pass onto the next contestant and say the same thing again but I stop her.

'Elaine,' I say, 'what happens now? It's ages until four o'clock.'

'You're free,' says Elaine. 'You need to be back here at half-two for hair and make-up. Other than that, the afternoon is yours! Go and enjoy London!'

I can't think of anything worse. My heart sinks into my black ballet pumps as I trudge out of the building and back into the hot, smelly streets of London. I haven't eaten a proper meal for over twenty-four hours and my head is throbbing.

I find a cafe nearby and order a fried egg on toast and a cup of tea but my throat seems to be closing up and cafes never seem to be able to cook a fried egg the way I like it. When I do them at home I use super-hot olive oil and cook the egg on a high heat, spooning the oil over the white to avoid that horrid jelly bit around the yolk. I like the edges nice and frizzled and crispy and the yolk soft and hot. This egg is all the wrong way round. The white is soggy and cold and the yolk has turned to thick yellow rubber. I find it hard to shove the greasy food down my throat and without Creon it's not going to get digested properly anyway, so in the end I give up and just have the tea.

I feel another mega-coughing session coming on, so I pay and leave the cafe straight away. Then I find a small square of green in the centre of the busy streets and sit on a bench. I hack my guts up, rattling and retching and gasping for breath and then everything goes kind of spinny, so I clutch at the edge of the bench and tell myself not to panic, but it's no good.

I'm really struggling for every breath now. I'm not sure how I'm going to even stand up straight, let alone get back to the TV studios and cook my three recipes again in front of the cameras for real this time.

I sit with my head buried in my hands, trying to think.

In the end I do the only thing I can think of doing.

The thing I didn't want to do at all.

I fumble in my jeans pocket and open my mobile phone.

Sticky German Gingerbread
with Vanilla Custard

For the gingerbread, you will need:
    230g (8oz) butter
    230g (8oz) soft brown sugar
    170g (6oz) golden syrup
    60g (2oz) black treacle
    340g (12oz) self-raising flour
    2 eggs, beaten
    2 level dessert spoons of ground ginger
    1 level dessert spoon of ground cinnamon
    A pinch of salt
    1 level teaspoon of bicarbonate of soda
    230ml (7 fl oz) warm milk

For the vanilla custard, you will need:

200ml (7oz) milk

200ml (7oz) double cream

1 vanilla pod, split seeds scraped out (you can find vanilla pods in the baking section of most supermarkets)

75g (2½oz) caster sugar

2 free-range egg yolks (you can use non free-range, but these do taste better and are much kinder to the hens)

Preheat the oven to 150°C/300°F/gas mark 2. Grease and line a two-pound loaf tin (or an 11 ½ x 7 ½ inch round tin) – you can line it with greaseproof paper which is easily found in the supermarket.

Get a large saucepan and slowly melt together the treacle, sugar and butter on a low heat. When the mixture is nice and gloopy, remove from the heat and stir in the beaten eggs. Sieve the flour, salt, cinnamon and ginger into the melted mixture. Sieve the bicarbonate of soda into a mixing bowl and pour the warm milk over it. Add this to the treacle mixture, stirring well to combine all the ingredients. Pour into the tin and bake for about 1 ½ hours.

Allow the gingerbread to cool in the tin before removing.

If you like the top of your gingerbread to be extra messy and sticky and delicious – which, let's face it, I do, because I'm obsessed with this stuff – then brush some more golden syrup over the top while the cake is still warm.

To make the vanilla custard, place the milk, cream and the vanilla pod and seeds into a saucepan on a low heat. Bring gently to the boil, then remove from the heat and remove the vanilla pod.

Whisk the sugar and egg yolks together in a large bowl with a hand whisk (or a fork if you haven't got one) until pale and frothy. Pour the egg mixture over the milk and cream and whisk together. Pour the mixture into a clean saucepan and continue whisking over a low heat until a frothy custard is formed. Then pour into a jug and serve with a big, thick slice of the German gingerbread.

Chapter Fourteen

Harry answers on the first ring. He never usually does that so I know I'm in trouble.

'Mel!' he says. 'Where are you? I've been trying to call you all morning.'

I sigh and swallow down great lumps of mucus in an effort to be able to talk to him. Just hearing his low, kind voice is making me want to sob for England.

'I'm in Bloomsbury,' I whisper, but still trying to be heard above the roar of traffic. 'I'm doing the competition, you know?'

'Yeah, I know,' says Harry. 'I didn't think you'd actually be stupid enough to go behind your mum's back. You do know that she's furious? And going out of her mind with worry?'

I sit up straight.

'You've spoken to her?' I say. 'Why?'

'Er, why do you think?' says Harry. 'You didn't come home last night. She thought you might be with me. Oh, and she spoke to Gemma after that and read your letter. So she knows exactly where you've gone.'

'Well, not exactly,' I mutter, flushing even though he can't see me. 'She can't know exactly.'

'Stop being an idiot,' says Harry in a voice quite unlike his normal mild one. 'She's in bits. You were supposed to be at the hospital now.'

'I know,' I whisper. 'I just had to do this competition. You know how much it means to me.'

'Well, yeah,' says Harry. 'I do. But maybe your mother should mean more to you?'

There's a silence while I digest the horribleness of what I've done.

'Anyway,' says Harry. 'She's in a bit of a state at home and your dad's with her. So I suggested that I come up to London and get you and we come home together on the train. The hospital says you can still be admitted tonight if you get a move on.'

I scowl against the blinding light of the sun. I'm sitting on a bench which has no shade whatsoever.

'I'm not coming home until I've done the competition,' I say. 'I'm here now and I've already done the rehearsal. Hold on.'

I cover the mouthpiece and bend over to cough. When I've finished there's a loud sigh from Harry on the other end of the line.

'Are you taking your medication?' he says. 'You sound dead rough.'

'Thanks,' I say, feebly. I hang onto the phone as if it were the last possession I'm ever going to have. I don't want to lose the feeling of Harry's voice in my ear, even if he IS cross with me.

'Have you had your pills today?' says Harry. He's not going to give up.

I wait a moment to make sure that I really need to say what I'm about to say, but then I go dizzy again and everything spins round.

'I lost my meds bag,' I say in a small voice. 'On the train. So I haven't had anything since yesterday afternoon.'

'Christ, Mel,' says Harry. He sounds as if he's going to burst a few major blood vessels. 'Why didn't you ring me? Or find a doctor? Or come home. Are you stupid or something?'

He's so angry that I melt into a puddle of insecurity and begin to cry.

'I just wanted to prove that I could do something,' I say in between sobs. 'I hate being the stupid girl with CF who can't do anything because she gets out of breath.'

That's a silly thing to say because now I'm so out of breath that I can't really talk.

'OK, so you've got to London on your own,' says Harry. 'Big frigging deal. And now you're in trouble so I'm coming to get you. I've promised your mum, anyway. Give me the name of the place you're staying at.'

He's not really going to take any more argument from

me. I can tell from the tone of his voice.

Harry takes down the name and address of the B&B and the TV studio.

'OK,' he says. 'I'm going to the station now. Should be with you by 2. I'll go to your house first and get the meds. Stay at the B&B and don't go anywhere, OK?'

'I need to be in hair and make-up at 2.30,' I say in a small protesting voice, but Harry makes a noise of disgust.

'Love you,' I say to the phone, but he's hung up.

I sit on the bench and the floodgates finally open.

I cry and cry and cry.

By the time it gets towards 2 I feel calmer.

I've decided what I'm going to do.

I'm going to ring Harry and tell him – tell, not ask – that I am going to do the competition whether he likes it or not. Then if I don't do well I will come home with him, and if I do we can both stay in the B&B and I will call Mum and tell her that I'm OK, but that I won't be having the operation.

I'm back in my room, sitting on the bed. I've changed into a prettier top with flowers on, but kept the same jeans. I've bought a new bottle of shampoo and washed my hair, even though it takes me about ten times longer than usual, because I have to keep stopping and leaning against the shiny white tiles of the bathroom wall to catch my breath.

I put on a smear of pink lipgloss to cover up my blue lips and survey myself in the mirror.

'Better,' I say. Then I double over and cough until

I'm sick. The next time I look in the mirror the lipgloss is smeared and my mascara has made damp black marks down my cheeks.

'Oh well,' I say. 'They're going to do my make-up anyway.'

I glance at my watch. It's just gone 2 now and I've got to get in a cab in the next five minutes or else I won't get to the studios in time.

Where's Harry?

I try his mobile a couple of times but it goes straight to voicemail. Then my phone rings while I'm holding it and I nearly drop it in fright. 'Mum' flashes up on the caller display, so I switch the phone right off in a panic and shove it back into my jeans. I can't cope with Mum's anger at the moment. She is so going to give me the biggest telling off known to man. Or girl. And if Dad gets hold of me I'm going to be toast – and not the lovely, crunchy white organic sort either, but the thin black charred variety made using rubbish sliced bread.

When it gets to 2.15 I can't wait any longer.

I get downstairs as fast as I can and run outside to hail a cab. The running is not a good idea but I can't be late for the quarter-finals of *Best Teen Baker*.

I just can't.

At 2.30 I'm sitting in a white-painted room full of gleaming mirrors and vases of red flowers. A lady called Chell, which I'm guessing might be short for Michelle, is puffing powder all over my face with a big soft brush.

'Anti-shine,' she says. 'Those TV lights can be very hot and unforgiving. Mind you, you've got lovely skin. Wish mine was as good.'

That's the first nice thing anybody's said to me about my appearance for ages and it makes me want to cry. Crying is so not a good thing to do when you have CF, as the illness already gives you blocked sinuses and crying screws up your breathing and I've already done too much of it today, so I wait until I'm sure my voice isn't going to wobble and I thank her.

'Sure I can't get you another drink, love?' she says, spraying my hair with some horrid chemical-smelling stuff. I grip my lips shut and try not to breathe any of it in. Everything in this make-up room is a potential cough hazard. 'I hear you've had the flu.'

I offer her a weak smile and shake my head. If only I did have the flu. If I had the flu it would go away in a few days and I'd be healthy again. If I had the flu my worried boyfriend wouldn't be travelling across the country to get me and my angry mother wouldn't be on the warpath of anxiety and rage.

'You do look a bit pale,' Michelle says, considering my face. 'Tiny bit more blush, don't you think?'

Actually I don't think. I already look like a peach that has been boiled in redcurrant juice. But she adds a bit more colour to my cheekbones and stands back to survey her handiwork.

'There,' she says. 'We've done a good job of covering up your lurgy!'

I snort and then try to cover it up by blowing my nose. If only she and everyone here knew the true story behind my 'lurgy'. Probably just as well they don't, or else I'd be in a London hospital bed right now and not about to enter the competition I've been waiting to get to for so long.

Underneath my excitement and nerves I feel so ill that I reckon I might just keel over and die at any point soon, but I'm determined to bake my chocolate fondants, my gingerbread and my biscuits and wow the judges with them first. Then at least I could die happy. Or part-happy, because actually I really want to get through to the semi-finals too.

'There isn't anybody waiting for me in reception, is there?' I say to Michelle. 'My boyfriend is supposed to be coming.'

Michelle sends another girl out down to reception to look, but she comes back and shakes her head.

'Oh well,' I say. 'He must have got stuck on a train somewhere.'

I feel disappointed and relieved all at the same time. I could do without him giving me a major lecture, but then again he's got all my meds and I need them like yesterday.

And if I saw Harry's sweet face, I know I'd cook the best I've ever cooked.

Just to make him proud of me again.

We're standing behind our cook stations primed for action.

The cameras begin to roll and the presenter of the programme steps forwards. He's a large man with a polished bald head and glasses and he's wearing a grey pin-striped suit. He looks more like a double-glazing salesman than the host of a cookery programme I reckon, but he's got a big grin and when we were all introduced to him just before the cameras began to roll, he took the trouble to have a chat with each of us in turn.

The man's got a camera pointing at him now and he introduces the programme and says a bit about the competition. Then some dramatic music comes pounding into the studio and the man holds his breath for a moment, looks up at us where we're standing in our aprons behind our cookers and then bellows out, 'ONE, TWO, THREE – LET'S BAKE!'

My legs go weak. I put the oven on, grease my cake tin, grab my mixing bowl and start tipping flour onto the scales.

Right. This is it. This is the day that will affect the rest of my life.

I start with the gingerbread as it takes longest to cook. I put butter and brown sugar in a vast steel saucepan, stirring with a wooden spoon until they melt into a smooth brown puddle, then I pour in the golden syrup and black treacle. When it's all broken down into a thick sticky mixture, I beat in a couple of large eggs. Then in the big mixing bowl next to me I put flour, powdered ginger, eggs, salt and cinnamon and then tip the whole lot into the glorious gooey treacle mix. I stir for ages to make sure all the ingredients are mixed in otherwise there will be uneven clumps of flour in the middle of the cake. The spicy, gingery buttery smell is like heaven. Then I fold in warm milk mixed with bicarbonate of soda until the texture changes from a sticky dark brown to pale, cappuccino-coloured foam, which begins to rise up towards the rim of the saucepan. I taste a spoonful and nod. It's ready. I pick up the pan and tip the rich frothy mixture into my prepared loaf tins and then I slam them into the oven on a medium heat to cook for just under an hour.

Macaroons next. I grease a baking tray with butter and line it with edible rice paper. Then I mix together my sugar, ground almonds and ground rice. I add some almond essence and an egg white and then beat the whole mixture until it's ready to be piped in little circles onto the rice paper. I add an almond to the top of each biscuit and can't resist popping one into my mouth. Uh-oh. Dumb idea. Nuts are not good when you are trying not to cough. I take a swig from my bottle of water and try to calm the choking feeling. Then I whiz the macaroons into the oven for twenty-five minutes. I wipe the sweat off my head with my right arm and make a mental note to trim the rice paper to fit each biscuit when they're baked.

Then I at last turn my attention to making the chocolate fondants. This is the most risky of my three dishes. The right cooking time is essential to get the runny chocolate centre inside the sponge. If you cook them too long they just become like chocolate cake instead.

I melt dark chocolate and butter together in a bowl over a saucepan of hot water. Then in a big brown mixing bowl I beat together my sugar, egg yolks, whole eggs and flour. I pour the melted chocolate mixture into this bowl and then fold in the flour with a large metal spoon. I scoop up a fingerful of mixture and test it. It's sweet, but with a slight undertone of bitterness from the cocoa-rich chocolate. Perfect. I dollop the chocolaty mix into six small round baking tins and put them into my pre-heated oven to cook for ten minutes.

All three dishes are in the oven. Result! These three recipes are definitely going to go into *The Amelie Day Book of Baking*. I reckon I've got them down to a fine art.

I steady myself on the worktop. My head is damp with sweat and my chest feels terrible but it's like I'm on another planet where nothing matters except the moment I'm in. I'm not even really aware of the other contestants, even though I can hear them slamming oven doors and clanking pans and hear the hiss of hot steam coming from all directions. The lights are so bright that I can't see anybody anyway.

I need to take my chocolate fondants out. I don't know whether the runny centre has worked but they've risen well and the deep dark chocolate smell makes my taste buds zing into action. I put them onto white plates and then I whisk vanilla and icing sugar into double cream to make the Chantilly crème to serve them with. I tip the cream into six tiny glasses to be put on each plate of chocolate fondant.

Then I add milk and cream into a saucepan for my vanilla custard and slice open a black vanilla pod with the tip of a sharp knife. My hands are shaking so much that

I have to take care not to slice off my fingers. I scrape the seeds from the pod onto the tip of my knife and then slide them into the mixture, bring it to the boil and tip cornflour, eggs and sugar into another bowl. I mix them together, tip the milk mix into the bowl and whisk it all together before transferring it all back into the pan. Then I leave the whole thing to cook for fifteen minutes, stirring nearly all the time until it is thick enough to coat the back of my silver spoon with thick, sweet, yellow custard. While it's bubbling I get my macaroons out and trim the rice paper so that it fits in a neat circle underneath each biscuit.

I'm boiling now. My face is dripping sweat and I feel dizzy, but all I can focus on is the food.

I wipe down all my surfaces to remove the mess of flour and butter and icing sugar. Then, while the custard is cooking, I take out my German gingerbread.

It looks brilliant. The cake is hot and soft, with a sticky topping where I brushed it with golden syrup before baking. I slice it and inhale the hot gingery steam but not enough to risk making myself cough – just a tiny sniff. Then I put a couple of slices on a white plate and I pour my thick yellow vanilla custard from the saucepan into a white jug and put this next to it. I dust white icing sugar over the top of the cake as a contrast even though I didn't rehearse it this way. It looks like fresh snowfall on dark earth. That's what I like best about cooking. You can make stuff up as you go along.

I stand back and wipe my forehead with the back of my sleeve.

And just in time.

'STOP COOKING!' yells the bald guy.

That's it. The two hours are up. They went so fast I hardly had time to breathe, which is not good when you have CF, as breathing is difficult even on a good day.

I glance around. Two of the other contestants are frantically trying to finish serving their meals.

I wash my hands, wipe the edges of my three plates of food with a tea towel so that there are no messy smudges and arrange them on the work surface in front of me, ready for judging. Then I try to calm my beating heart, which is difficult when you have CF, because the usual way of taking deep steadying breaths is not really an option.

The presenter starts to make his way around all twelve of the contestants with the judges. I reckon I'm about sixth in line to be interviewed, so I have time to stand and catch my breath and steady myself against the granite work top before they get to me.

Then there's kind of a commotion behind the camera.

I try not to look because we're supposed to be standing calm and collected behind our workstations and not gawping towards the camera, but I can't help it.

The lights in here are very bright. All I can see is a pair of arms waving in the air as if in the middle of an argument and then Elaine, the floor manager, comes up just behind the camera so she can't be seen on TV and she beckons me to come off the floor.

I look left and right just in case she means one of the other contestants but she's definitely pointing at me.

My heart sinks. I step down from the workstation and leave all my lovely gleaming pots and pans behind. My three dishes sit ready for the judges and they look really good. Why am I being called off? I don't look THAT ill, surely? Michelle did a good job in make-up.

Then I'm hustled behind the cameras and out of the studio into a little room.

She leaps up and comes towards me with her face pale and her arms outstretched.

'Mum!' I say. 'What are you doing here?'

Then another figure comes out from behind her.

It's my father. And he reaches out to hug me too.

I'm more scared than I've ever been in my life.

There's something terribly wrong with their faces.

They're not angry for a start.

My mother holds onto me so tight that I start to suffocate and have to pull my face out of her soft cashmere top.

'Oh Amelie,' she says. 'Sit down. We need to talk to you. In private.'

Chapter Fifteen

I sit down with my parents one on either side of me. They each take one of my hands.

'Stop it,' I say. 'You're scaring me! Why aren't you angry? Harry said you were angry!'

Mum glances at Dad. She's trying not to cry.

'We have to tell you something,' she says. 'Don't worry. It will be alright.'

She gets up and goes and stares out of the window at the busy street outside. I recognise Dad's car parked outside on a yellow line.

'Why've you come in the car?' I say. 'Wouldn't the train have been easier?'

'We wanted to get here as fast as we could,' says Dad.

I look at Mum. She looks in one piece, despite the fact that she's crying into a tissue.

'Who – what?' I say, confused. 'Why isn't Harry here? He should have been here ages ago. He was coming to get me. Why – oh, no. Please don't tell me that. PLEASE DON'T TELL ME.'

I start to shake. I stare at my parents wide-eyed. Why aren't they speaking? Shouldn't they be reassuring me that Harry is fine, that he's outside in the car waiting for us or at home waiting for me to come back from London?

Somehow my parents don't need to speak. Their eyes and ashen faces are telling me everything I so don't want to know.

'What happened?' I say. I feel as if I need to hold it together or I'm going to start to yell and scream and never stop.

'He was rushing to get a train,' says Dad. 'He stepped out on Station Road without looking, from what we can gather. White van was going too fast, couldn't stop in time. He's in Redhill hospital.'

I stare at Dad, not understanding.

'Do you mean... he's not... you know?' I say. I can't bring myself to say the word in case saying it makes it happen. A vision of Harry's curly dark brown hair and brown eyes flashes in front of my eyes. I've always liked the freckles across the bridge of his nose and the way that his eyes seem to get darker when he's serious about something.

We've all got to die sometime, right? Any of us could die tomorrow.

The tears are coming now. Mum comes over and gives me a tissue. Then she holds a bowl underneath my mouth while I cough myself almost unconscious.

'He's critical,' she says. 'His parents are at his bedside. That's why we've come to get you. We need to get there as soon as possible but I have to warn you, Amelie. We may not make it in time.'

I get up.

'What are we waiting for?' I say. 'I've got to see Harry. I've got to.'

Then we leave the TV studios without ever looking back.

In the car Mum sits in the back while Dad drives.

She passes me an inhaler and a nebuliser and tells me to use them. Then she hooks me up to an oxygen canister and I take deep steadying breaths until at last the tightness in my chest calms down a bit and my breath comes more easily.

Then she forces me to eat a sandwich and some Creon followed by a milkshake and a bar of chocolate. I feel as if eating is the last thing I ever want to do again, but I know that there's to be no argument. It's such a relief to have my meds back again and to feel like I'm not about to keel over and pass out, anyway.

I lean back against the seat and close my eyes for the entire journey back. I'm not asleep, but I'm thinking about all the good things that Harry has done for me since we were little and I'm replaying them over and over while silent tears pour down my cheeks.

When we pull up at the gates of the local hospital I sit up. My heart starts to pound and I feel shaky.

'You'll come in with me, won't you?' I say to Mum.

'Even though you're probably really angry with me.'

Mum sighs and wipes the tears from my cheeks with her tissue.

'Well, I was,' she says. 'But then I was so relieved to know where you were. You should never have done this, Amelie. You should never have travelled to London in the state that you were in. You should never have run off when you were booked in for an operation. And you should NEVER have lied to me and your father and poor Harry in the way that you did.'

She does still sound a bit angry underneath the weariness. I wish she hadn't said that last bit, but the thing is, it's true.

If I hadn't gone to London and lied, Harry wouldn't have tried to rush after me.

He'd still be at school playing rugby or leaping about on the tennis courts.

If anything happens to him... if anything happens to Harry, it's all my fault. I'll never forgive myself. Never.

The three of us walk into the hospital foyer in silence.

Harry's parents are sitting one on either side of his bed as we come in.

Mum and Dad go straight over to them and offer hugs of sympathy. Our parents have been friends for many years.

I try not to look at Harry. There's a mass of tubes and machines all over him.

'Hello, Mel,' says Harry's father. He's always been kind

to me, ever since I was a little girl and he lived next door. I like his grey hair and black glasses and the way he's holding Harry's hand. 'Come and sit by the bed.'

I look at his mother. She's staring at me but the expression on her face is difficult to read. Except that I can read it, or at least I think I can. It says:

You've got a nerve, turning up here. If it wasn't for your stupid selfish trip to London, my boy would still be at home doing his homework or out playing rugby. You don't deserve to be here at his bedside. I wish to God you hadn't come.

I stare at my feet.

'Come,' says Harry's father, holding out his hand to me. 'It's OK.'

I look at Mum and Dad behind me and they nod and then fade off back out into the hospital corridor. There aren't supposed to be more than two visitors by the bed at a time, but that still leaves three of us.

'I'll go and get some coffee,' says Harry's mum. She stands up and stretches her back with a grimace. Her face is streaked with tears and make-up. 'Let me know straight away if anything changes, Adam.'

She walks past me taking care not to brush against me. Probably just as well. I feel that feeble that I'd probably fall to the floor. Mum says that I've got to go to the CF centre on the way home and get checked out. She reckons I've got another chest infection and I think she might be right. We haven't yet touched on the sensitive subject of the operation I was supposed to be having this morning.

Harry's dad gestures at the empty chair next to his

bed. I creep into it, feeling awkward and shaken to the core. I can't very well not look at Harry with his dad right there, so I turn and look down at his face. Most of it is obscured by tubes in his mouth, tubes up his nose and a large bandage right round the top of his head. His eyes are shut and what I can see of his face is bruised and cut and bloody.

It's all wrong seeing big, healthy, red-cheeked Harry in a hospital bed. Somebody might as well have picked up a load of earth and thrown it onto the soft white pillows.

'He looks like he's asleep,' I say and then I curse myself straight away. I'm such an idiot. If he was asleep he'd hardly be covered in all this medical stuff, would he?

'Well, he kind of is,' says Harry's father. His voice has a little shake in it and he is being careful to keep his voice measured and kind. 'Unfortunately he's in a coma. That's a little more serious.'

I flush and nod. I feel like a spare part.

'You can hold his hand if you like,' says Adam. 'And you can talk to him. You never know, he might be able to hear it somehow.'

I take Harry's limp hand in my own. It's cool and soft. Then I clear my throat and prepare to say something, but it's really embarrassing with Harry's father sitting right opposite.

As if he senses this, Adam gets up and gives me a smile. Then he heads outside and I see him put his arm around Harry's mother and persuade her to stay in the corridor for a moment.

I wait until the door has closed and then I put Harry's hand to my cheek and hold it there in silence for moment.

You know when you just kind of assume that somebody is going to be in your life forever? Well, I thought that Harry and I would be going out for the rest of our lives and that we might one day even get married. When we stopped being little friends who played football together and he asked me out, my mother gave me the CF Police lecture about how I shouldn't get too hung up on my first ever boyfriend, because first loves never lasts and I should put my health first and all that stuff. Then when we got to a year of going out and then two, my parents decided to accept that we were pretty serious about each other and they even invited Harry on holiday with us last year. I've been on holiday with his family too and we've all had dinner together either at his house or ours.

Harry is part of the fabric of my life.

And he gets my CF. He never makes me feel bad about it or inadequate and although he fusses a bit about my medication it's only 'cos he loves me.

Part of me wishes I'd told Harry I was going to London in the first place, but if I had he'd only have tried to stop me.

It all seems a bit stupid now, my obsession with baking and cakes.

I put a load of sponge, eggs and butter ahead of my own boyfriend and my family and I lied to them and worried them and left them behind, just so that I could enter a stupid competition.

'I'm sorry, Harry,' I whisper into his cold hand. 'I'm so,

so sorry. I'm the most rubbish girlfriend in the universe and I quite understand if you want to dump me pronto when you wake up.'

That's if he does wake up. The doctors told Mum that it's quite likely he'll never regain consciousness and that his parents will have to make the heartbreaking decision to turn off his life-support machine.

I'm trying not to think about that option.

This is Harry. MY Harry. My big, cheerful, red-cheeked, floppy-haired Harry.

He's not going anywhere while I've got a say in the matter.

'I've got to go,' I whisper. Harry's mother is hovering outside the door looking anguished. 'Your mum's coming to sit with you now. But I'll be back tomorrow.'

I give him a kiss on the forehead and go outside to where my parents are sitting in the corridor on orange plastic chairs.

They spring up when I come out.

'Not easy for you, love,' says Mum. She puts her arms around me. 'But we need to go and get you checked out now. The last thing we all need is you getting sicker again.'

I bury my head into her chest and sob dry, painful sobs mixed with retching coughs. Dad rubs my back in silence. These have been the worst two days of my life, apart from that bit where I did my recipes for the competition. That bit felt good. But it's not real life. Real life is Mum, Dad, Harry and me.

And CF.

~

Turns out I'm actually quite ill.

I see another consultant at the CF centre because Mr Rogers is on holiday and as soon as she's examined me and listened to my cough she tells Mum that to be safe, they're going to admit me until this infection clears.

I try to protest but I've got a fever and I'm all shivery and super-tired so I don't argue all that much. It's kind of a relief to be tucked up in the soft white hospital bed. I've got antibiotics being pumped into my system and I'm quite dehydrated after London, so I'm hooked up on a fluid drip as well.

The only thing I hate about it is that I'm not allowed out of bed to go and see Harry.

On the third day I have an operation to put the gastrostomy into my stomach.

I have to be put to sleep for that so when I wake up I'm groggy and a bit sore, but the first thing I ask Mum is if there is any news of Harry and she shakes her head.

'No change,' she says. 'Sorry. I know that's not what you want to hear.'

I lie on my thick hospital pillows and let the tears trickle down my face with my eyes closed. Mum sits next to me and holds my hand until I go to sleep.

The next time I wake up Dad is sitting by the bed.

'What day is it?' I say, confused. The blinds in the room are drawn so I can't tell.

'Same day you had your op,' says Dad. 'Evening. They've said you can go home tomorrow, Mel. That's great news, isn't it?'

I smile because it's what he wants me to do, but underneath I feel sad and hollow. I can't imagine what going home and not being with Harry is going to feel like. All I can see stretching out ahead of me is grief and loneliness and the continuing burden of my CF as it gets worse and worse.

'I feel rubbish,' I say to Dad. He nods.

'Your mum will have you feeling right as rain,' he says. 'Oh, and she's got some news for you. I'll let her tell you herself.'

I prop myself up into a sitting position with a grimace. I've got a small scar where the gastrostomy and the button which closes it off are and it tugs and pulls when I bend.

Mum comes in smiling with a bunch of yellow daffodils. She arranges these in the vase by my bed and then perches on it, her eyes twinkling.

'What?' I say. 'Is it Harry? Has he woken up?'

Mum chews her lip.

'Oh, sorry, no,' she says. 'I wish I could tell you that. But it's something you might quite like to hear anyway.'

'Are you getting back with Dad?' I say. That would be weird, but good.

'Oh, sorry, no,' says Mum again. 'We're getting on fine, which is a good reason not to live with one another again.'

'Well, what then?' I say. This is turning into a tiring question-and-answer game.

Then she tells me.

She's heard from the TV company who make *Best Teen*

Baker. They said that the judges were so impressed with the three dishes I left behind when I rushed off that they've put me through to the semi-finals.

'They said that you had managed to pull off the perfect chocolate fondant,' says Mum. 'When they cut into it you could hear gasps of delight from the other judges when the chocolate oozed out of the middle!'

She's nearly bouncing up and down on the bed. My wound feels hot and sore. I have to put out a hand and stop her with a pained look.

'Oh,' I say, cautious. 'But haven't I missed the filming for the semi-finals?'

'Nope,' says Mum, all smug. 'They've said they'll postpone it until you're fit to travel. And this time I can come with you.'

I force out a small smile but my insides are aching with love and pain for Harry so it's a bit difficult to look too excited.

'I can't go,' I say. 'How can I leave Harry? I just can't go.'

Mum's smile fades, but then she nods and takes my hand.

'Never mind, love,' she says. 'It was great to be praised by the judges in that way. You should be proud.'

We chat on about the competition a bit, but underneath I feel anything but proud.

I made my sweet, kind, boyfriend rush up to London to rescue me and then he got run over.

How can I ever feel proud of myself again?

Chapter Sixteen

When I get out of hospital I rest at home for a couple of days.

Trish comes to the house and shows me and Mum how to hook a tube to my gastrostomy so that I can be given night feeds of extra calories while I'm asleep. At first I can't sleep because I swear I can feel the liquid going into me. The tube feed always has to be switched off at four in the morning and flushed through and disconnected, and the tubes from the oxygen canister feel uncomfortable as well, so I guess that's it for ever getting a decent night's sleep again. But I get used to the gastrostomy quite fast, so I don't feel quite as depressed about that, at least. Even after two days I weigh a bit more on the scales, so I'm really pleased, and so is Mum, but this horrid sadness drags me down every waking moment of the day.

I go back to school and Gemma makes sure that I don't get over-tired and she tells anybody who says anything nasty about me to back off and for once they do. Everybody knows about Harry. He was one of the most popular boys in his year, so I get a fair few people coming up to me and asking how he's doing.

I always tell them the same thing: 'He's alive, which is the main thing.'

But he hasn't come out of the coma.

I go out every lunch break and sit with Gemma under the old oak tree where I used to sit with Harry and sometimes we chat and at other times I'm silent and don't feel much like talking and she's fine with that. I feel guilty for feeling resentful of her health. She's a good friend – the best. And she's always there for me. So I tell her how I'm feeling and she nods and holds my hand.

And then.

I'm back working in Karim's shop.

He's agreed to start paying me my wages in money. Every time I think about baking (which let's face it, used to be pretty much 24/7), I get a big pang of sadness and anxiety in the pit of my stomach and I picture Harry's pale face on the hospital pillow and I know that it's all my fault he's there.

So I stop baking.

I stop reading cookery books and watching cookery programmes. I empty out all my ingredients cupboards at home and chuck a lot of it away.

Mum watches me with a sad look in her eye but doesn't dare speak. I'm on a short fuse, what with the worry about Harry and the plunge in my own health.

I no longer fill my basket with flour, eggs and sugar in Karim's shop. He counts out the notes at the end of the day and puts them into my hand with a sad look in his eyes.

'It's no good, Little Girl Who Bakes not baking,' he says. 'No good at all.'

'You're just saying that because it costs you more to pay me money,' I say with a sad smile, but he's not having any of it and goes back to the cash till shaking his head and making a noise which sounds like 'I, I, I' so I pocket the money and head towards home. Not sure what I'm going to do with my wages yet. Maybe I'll have to go clothes shopping with Gemma more often.

When I get in after my third day back at the shop, Mum's right on me the second I open the front door.

'Hospital rang,' she says, all out of breath. She shoves a coat in my direction and grabs her keys from the hall table. 'We've got to get there. Now.'

Mum won't say anything on the way. She drives quite fast and I swear she makes a speed camera flash but she just mutters a rude word, pulls a face and carries on at the same speed.

'He's not – he's not…' I say, unable to get the words out. I look at Mum's face. She doesn't look as if anybody has died. Then again it's sometimes hard to tell with Mum.

'Oh – no,' she says. 'Sorry. I didn't mean to worry you.'

We pull into the hospital car park and Mum grabs my hand and almost pulls me at a run towards the entrance foyer and then remembers that I find it kind of hard to breathe and I've just got out of hospital myself, so she slows down to a pounding walk.

I'm still really panting and coughing by the time we get up to the fifth floor.

Mum propels me past a smiling nurse and a smiling consultant in a white coat. Another smiling nurse comes out of Harry's room and almost claps her hands when she sees me. Everybody seems to have gone into slow motion for some reason. I have time to notice the gold filling in her front tooth when she smiles and the white name badge with black lettering on her blue uniform.

Harry's parents leap up when they see me come in. They're both smiling too. His mother looks about twenty years younger and quite pretty.

'Oh, Amelie,' she says. 'He's woken up! Quick – come and see.'

I'm already in tears.

Adam vacates his chair for me and I sit down and find myself staring straight into Harry's deep brown eyes.

'Hi,' I croak. I turn away and cough for a moment. Mum offers a bowl but I shake my head and turn back to Harry. He blinks at me and a slow smile spreads over his face. He's still wired up to machines and tubes, but this time his grip on my hand is strong and warm.

'He won't be able to say much,' warns his mother. 'But

164

he's back with us. That's what counts.'

She blows her nose and rests her cheek on Adam's shoulder. I can hear my own mother sniffling behind me.

'Cup...' says Harry, or at least something that sounds like that. 'Cup...'

He reaches up with his right hand and removes the oxygen mask from his face.

I frown and bend right down so that my head is near his mouth.

'Try it again,' I say. 'I'm listening.'

Harry summons up all his strength.

'Cupcakes,' he says.

'What did he say?' says his mother. 'I swear he just said "cupcakes"! But that can't be right.'

I laugh through my tears.

'Yeah, it is,' I say. 'My chocolate cupcakes. They're kind of like his favourites?'

'Oh,' says his mother, relaxing. 'That's OK then. For a moment there I thought he'd lost his mind in the accident.'

Later on they go out and leave me alone with Harry. He goes to sleep, but it's kind of nice listening to him breathe and knowing that he's going to wake up again. The doctors say that his recovery is going to take a long, long time and that he might have to learn how to walk all over again, but at least he's heading in the right direction now.

On the way home I'm quiet, chewing it all over in my head.

'I might do that competition after all,' I say from the passenger seat, where I'm eating a Mars Bar and a packet

165

of crisps. 'I think that Harry would want me to do it.'

'You're right there,' says Mum. 'But I'm coming with you this time, Amelie. No more running away to London and giving me a heart attack.'

I turn to look at my mum. I see her tired face and the lines underneath her eyes that have come from worrying about and caring for me every single day of my CF life. I realise something else, too. She's scared. One day she's going to have to face losing me for good and she's scared.

'I'm really sorry, Mum,' I say. 'I shouldn't have put my own stupid obsession ahead of how you're feeling. I promise I won't let it happen again.'

Mum laughs.

'You're a teenager!' she says. 'Of course it will happen again.'

When I get home I log onto my blog for the first time in a while.

Loads of people have caught on to what I was planning to do and have wished me good luck for the competition. Part of me wants to give a spoon-by-spoon account of the competition and what I cooked and how it turned out, but that seems a bit insensitive given that my boyfriend is in hospital and my parents are going to have to learn to trust me all over again. So instead I write a short paragraph explaining that I went to the competition, but my boyfriend was in an accident. Then I write this:

Thanks for all your nice posts and recipes. There seem

to be a load of big hurdles ahead of me. I've got loads of schoolwork to catch up on for exams next year. Anyway, Harry's going to take a very long time to get better. The doctors say that he will be in a wheelchair and have to miss a lot of school. I reckon he'll get really down now he can't play sports any longer. He's spent years being my support system and now I'm going to have to learn to be his. It seems kind of ironic that he's now going to be sick too and I'll have to take care of him. I get the feeling that this is going to take a lot more than just a box of cakes. And behind all this is the threat of my lung transplant. I could be waiting for years, or I could get a call any day now. Nobody really knows. And even if I did get new lungs, the doctors have warned me that my body might reject them and I'd be back to square one. And while I'm waiting to get the new lungs I could go downhill fast and end up in hospital for good. I might even die if my lung function drops any further.

I screw up my face against all these scary thoughts. I wish for about the millionth time that I could just be a normal teenager worrying about exams and spots and boys. I don't know how I'm going to cope with life now that I've removed my great passion of baking from it. I've just realised that apart from Harry, baking was the only thing which really helped me cope with my CF. I reckon I was maybe a bit hasty throwing out all my ingredients. A future without Flour Power looms ahead of me, looking bleak and boring and kind of – uncooked.

I look back at the screen and type some more.

But maybe I need to cook myself past the semi-finals of *Best Teen Baker* if I want to achieve my life's ambition of getting to the final and maybe even winning. After all, I live to bake. If I stop baking, I might stop living. And please carry on sending your recipes. I might ask to borrow them for my best-selling book of the future, *The Amelie Day Book of Baking*.

I snap the computer shut.

A vision of Harry floats in front of my eyes.

'Mum,' I say, going downstairs. 'Can you give me a lift to Karim's shop?'

Mum's sitting over the newspaper downstairs. She takes off her glasses and rubs her eyes. Her skin looks dry and tired and her eyes are like slits from lack of sleep.

'What do you want to buy?' she says. 'We've got loads of food in the kitchen.'

I roll my eyes and give her an impatient smile.

'I've got to do Harry's cupcakes,' I say. 'I need chocolate, eggs, flour and butter, like NOW.'

My mother's face lights up and sparkles in the late afternoon sun.

She grabs the car keys and we head outside.

Harry's Favourite Chocolate Heart Cupcakes

To make 12 of these gorgeous chocolatey treats, you will need:

    200g (7oz) self-raising flour
    225g (8oz) caster sugar
    25g (1oz) cocoa powder
    100g (3 ½ oz) margarine/butter
    2 medium eggs
    5 tablespoons of evaporated milk or normal milk
    5 tablespoons of water

To decorate:

    A family-sized bar of milk chocolate
    A small ball of ready-to-roll fondant icing and scarlet food colouring, or chocolate buttons, sprinkles, Jelly Tots or Smarties

Preheat the oven to 180°C/360°F/gas mark 4. Although I call these 'cupcakes' if you make them in muffin tins they turn out bigger, which can't be bad! Put 12 muffin cases into the tin and set aside for later.

Put the margarine/butter into a bowl with the caster sugar and cream these together with a wooden spoon until smooth. Then beat in the eggs, one at a time. Sieve the flour and then add to this mix, beating in until you have a smooth mixture. Then add your cocoa powder (you can add a bit more than 25g (1oz) if you like a stronger chocolate flavour, but I find that this amount is usually about right).

Add in 5 tablespoons of normal milk (if you like your cakes light and springy) or instead, you could use 5 tablespoons of evaporated milk (this gives a much creamier, moister texture, which I think is better). Then finally, add 5 tablespoons of water and beat the mixture until you have a lovely rich, brown chocolate mix.

Spoon the mixture into your prepared muffin tins so that each case is about three quarters filled (the mixture might make more than 12). Slide the tray into the middle of your heated oven and bake for about 20 minutes or until risen and firm.

You can either ice the cakes with icing sugar and water mixed together (and any food colouring you might like to add), or you can do what I like best – melt a family-sized bar of milk chocolate in a bowl over a pan of simmering water, then brush the chocolate all over the top of each little cake.

Harry is very fussy about cupcakes. I once put a red fondant icing heart on one of his cakes and ever since then he kind of expects it. If you like getting your hands covered in food colouring and making a squidgy mess on the worktop, then you could add some drops of scarlet food colouring to a small ball of ready-to-roll fondant icing. Roll it in your hands until you've got a ball of pinkish dough, roll it out with a rolling pin and then use a tiny heart-shaped cutter to cut out a pink heart. But be warned, your hands will look like something out of a horror film afterwards.

Or if you actually don't want to spend hours messing around with hearts, a much easier way to top off the milk chocolate on your cakes is to buy some chocolate buttons or similar and just stick one on top of each cake. Or you could get chocolate sprinkles, or Jelly Tots, or Smarties, or nearly anything you fancy putting on top.

These need to be kept in an airtight tin after they've cooled down. But in our house, they never last that long!

Author's note

The Baking Life of Amelie Day is a work of fiction based upon my own particular research. It is important to note that Cystic Fibrosis affects different people in different ways. I wrote this book after watching a television documentary about CF. It followed a group of young people who were waiting for life-saving lung transplants and I was touched by the daily struggles they had just to stay alive. Cystic Fibrosis is a life-shortening genetic condition which slowly destroys the lungs and digestive system, and there's currently no cure. Only half of sufferers live to celebrate their 40th birthday. To find out more about Cystic Fibrosis you can contact the Cystic Fibrosis Trust at www.cysticfibrosis.org.uk or call the CF Trust helpline on 0300 373 1000. You may also like to follow the blog of Victoria Tremlett who lives with CF at www.tor-pastthepointofnoreturn.blogspot.co.uk. Some of my research was aided by Oliver Jackson, who lives with CF, and I'd like to thank him for his input.

About the author

Vanessa is the award-winning author of several young adult novels including *Zelah Green* (Egmont, 2009), which won the Manchester Children's Book Prize and was shortlisted for the Waterstones Prize 2009, and *The Haunting of Tabitha Grey* (Egmont, 2012), a contemporary ghost story with a shocking twist.

More titles from Curious Fox

The adventures of Rémy Brunel

No one performs on the circus trapeze like
Rémy Brunel. But Rémy also leads another life,
prowling through the backstreets of Victorian
London as a jewel thief. Forced by the evil
circus owner Gustave to attempt the theft of
one of the world's most valuable diamonds,
she discovers an underworld of treachery
and fiendish plots.

*I was holding my breath ... I never
expected what happened to happen*

Stormi, Books, Movies, Reviews! Oh My! blog

The Serpent House

Twelve-year-old Annie is invited to Hexer Hall
to work as a servant for the mysterious Lady
Hexer. Carvings of snakes are everywhere and
when Annie touches one, she travels back in time
to when the Hall was a leper hospital, run by a
sinister doctor with a collection of
terrifying serpents.

*A chilling time-slip story with a strong sense
of the past, full of magic and mystery*

Lovereading4kids

For more exciting books from
brilliant authors, follow the fox!

www.curious-fox.com

'An unforgettable journey into a hauntingly imagined near-future. With her **mind-bending vision, breathtaking storytelling and utterly original voice**, Claire Vaye Watkins is one of my favorite writers'   Ruth Ozeki, author of *A Tale for the Time Being*

'An extraordinary novel: **relentlessly brilliant, utterly fearless, and often savagely funny**. Watkins explores the maze of human thirst in all its forms. Here's a love story that tracks the mutating hopes of two lost souls, in prose that is fever-bright and ferociously assured. More confirmation that **Watkins is one of the brightest stars in our firmament**'   Karen Russell, author of *Swamplandia* and *Vampires in the Lemon Grove*

'Like the best stories in her 2013 Dylan Thomas Prize-winning collection *Battleborn*, the narrative focuses on left-behind people and left-behind places – those who exist at the periphery of destructive events ... Which may make it surprising to say that this book is also funny. It's funny in the way that a Joy Williams or Mary Gaitskill or Flannery O'Connor story is funny. **It's laughter in the dark, the comedy of unending struggle ... The sentences in *Gold Fame Citrus* are alive** in ways the sun-blasted landscape isn't, and therein lies the hope'   Jonathan Lee, *Financial Times*

'The empty swimming pools and intense light conjure J. G. Ballard's environmental dystopias as well as Margaret Atwood's ... Both nail-biting and digressive, at times lushly overwritten, at times wryly incisive, but always powerful ... Vaye Watkins' portrait of Levi, the leader of the sand dune colony, is **a tour de force**: chilling, beguiling, paranoid, convincing and pathetic by turns ... Her novel certainly **cuts deep in its vision of overwhelming natural power** ... most of all in her extraordinary creation of the dune sea ... too vast for human comprehension, yet at the same time a tabula rasa for each fragile individu...   c sublime, **as mesm...   , *Guardian*

90710 000 296 500

'A wild book conveying the allure of people improvising, as well as the strange charm of the landscape ... Vaye Watkins is well versed in the region's seductive myths ... It is hard not to read the demise of idealogy as well as collapsing ecology as the driving force – a contemporary distrust of power, whoever wields it. Even her pleasure in language reflects back a suspicion of rhetoric that seeks to persuade ... The complexities of emotion and power are probed so intelligently'   Kate Webb, *Times Literary Supplement*

'California has always been the place where they went to start it big. Lured by 'gold, fame, citrus' as a character puts it, a phrase on which her book is a fascinating, dystopian fugue ... Like McCarthy, her desert landscapes are dense as well as barren, not just in the physical detail with which they're rendered, but the significance with which characters imbue them ... **A powerful portrait of an apocalypse less the result of external catastrophe, than familiar human failings'**
Sam Kitchener, *Independent*

'Watkins's **apocalyptic new novel seems a revisionist refit of McCarthy's** *The Road* ... that (unlike *The Road*) puts female characters centre-stage in a geographically vivid setting ... Formidably wrought'
Anthony Cummins, *Daily Telegraph*

'Watkins writes with **grace, wit and imagination** in her first novel ... Watkins's writing engrosses because she is mainly concerned with how people behave in extreme circumstances; no matter how strange the background, her characters stay believable'
Kate Saunders, *The Times*

'American odyssey: Set in a drought-ravaged Southern California trolled by scavengers, *Gold Fame Citrus* burns with a **dizzying, scorching genius'**   *Vanity Fair*

BY CLAIRE VAYE WATKINS

Battleborn: stories

Gold Fame Citrus